VOICES IN THE WATER

VOICES IN THE WATER

COLLECTED STORIES

EDWARD HOWER

Copyright © 2001 by EDWARD HOWER.

ISBN #:   Softcover   1-4010-3877-8

All rights reserved. No part of this book may be reproduced or transmitted in any form or by any means, electronic or mechanical, including photocopying, recording, or by any information storage and retrieval system, without permission in writing from the copyright owner.

This is a work of fiction. Names, characters, places and incidents either are the product of the author's imagination or are used fictitiously, and any resemblance to any actual persons, living or dead, events, or locales is entirely coincidental.

Cover Photo: Edward Hower
Author Photo: Claire McNamee

This book was printed in the United States of America.

To order additional copies of this book, contact:
Xlibris Corporation
1-888-7-XLIBRIS
www.Xlibris.com
Orders@Xlibris.com

Contents

VOICES IN THE WATER	11
ZEROES	23
THE EDUCATED BILLY-GOATS	45
KIKUYU WOMAN	64
GIVE ME TIME	85
MIRIAMU AND THE KING	104
SUPERBALL	119
THE OASIS	133
NIGHT OWL	146
THE FLYING PRINCESS	164
COUNTRY GARDENS	171
PEBBLES	192
THE TURQUOISE BALLOON	195
WHITE HIGHLANDS	210
AN AMOROUS CONSPIRACY	220
LADY OF THE LAKE	232
AT SARATOGA, 1985	246

for

Dan

and for

Lana

Most of the stories in this collection originally appeared, sometimes in slightly different forms, in *Atlantic Monthly, Epoch, Southern Review, Greensboro Review, Pleiades, Rockhurst Review, Transition* (Ghana), *Chapel Hill Advocate* (PEN Syndicated Fiction Award), *Mississippi Valley Review* (20th Anniversary Award), *Ithaca Times, New Novel Review, Cornell Review, Transatlantic Review* (UK), and *Shankpainter*.

VOICES IN THE WATER

One evening, Mary Dogflower, a 16-year old Iroquois girl, disappeared from her room. The other girls found her sitting cross-legged on the floor beside the water fountain in the building's foyer downstairs. She refused to move. Steven Fox, her staff counselor, found her there in the morning when he arrived at work.

Various staff members of the reform school tried to talk to her. She held her long straight hair in both fists against her cheeks and said nothing, When the girls gathered around her, she was silent with them, too. She sat absolutely motionless, her gaze never wandering from a fixed spot on the floor. Inez and Pam tried to get her interested in watching the dance rehearsal. Peaches told her how sad the group was going to feel if she didn't join them. Ronnie and Whale told her that if anybody had been calling her a dumb redskin again she ought to tell them and they'd kick some butts. Katrina told her she'd share a candy bar with her if she'd come upstairs. Mary pulled the frayed hem of her dress over her ankles. Her round face remained impassive. Finally she raised her eyes and stared at Katrina.

"My father's going to come and take me back to the reservation where I belong," she said.

Steven dispersed the girls. Dance rehearsal went on without Mary, as did the evening extra-credit classes in Spanish and shorthand. At 9:30, when it was time for evening chores, Mary was still refusing to move. She had settled into the corner between the water fountain and the wall, her head resting against the chrome edge of the box. She looked as if she were asleep with her eyes open.

Steven told the girls to do their chores and get into their bathrobes. There would be an emergency group therapy session at 10:15 in the foyer by the water fountain. He got Mary's case record out and looked through it in the staff office.

"You trying to find out if she's crazy?" Katrina, looking very skinny in her jeans and purple T-shirt, stood watching him in the doorway.

Steven tugged at his mustache, frowning. He had just found an observation report from a state hospital: "Subject manifests occasional mild schizophrenic behavior, catatonic type." He tossed the file onto the desk and straightened his tie. "Let's go try and talk to her, Katrina," he said.

The emergency group session was not a success. The girls sat on the floor in their fuzzy bathrobes and slippers and tried to talk to Mary. She wouldn't say a word. Everyone smoked cigarettes and looked at her. She looked at the tile next to her ankle. Her silence hung over the circle of girls like a drone. The girls couldn't take the pressure; they sighed loudly and made joking remarks. Mary looked quite peaceful, almost radiant, like the guest of honor at a party. At 11:30, Steven announced that she would be allowed to stay downstairs until morning, or until she wanted to come up to bed. He asked a group member to volunteer to take mattresses downstairs and stay with her.

The next morning, Mary was still sitting beside the water fountain. She had her dirty blanket covering all of her except her face, and didn't take it off all day. Girls volunteered to take watches sitting with her. Several staff visited with her, and eventually walked away shaking their heads. The school director sat with her for fifteen minutes.

"Did she say anything to you?" Steven asked him, when he had returned to his office.

"Yes." The director frowned over the top of his glasses. "She said that her father was going to come and take her back to the reservation where she belonged."

Another emergency group was held after dinner until bedtime. Mary did not speak. At one point, there was a moment of hope; the girls cheered and clapped—Mary stood up. She lumbered off with everyone watching. But she was merely taking one of her trips to the bathroom down the hall. She returned, had a long drink of water from the fountain, and resumed her silent sitting position.

After two nights and two days, Steven decided that if she was still there the next morning, he would have to have her picked up bodily and taken to the mental hospital for observation. As a last resort, he mentioned this to Katrina, who had volunteered to spend the night with Mary.

"What do I get if she comes upstairs?" Katrina asked.

Steven tilted back in his chair. The usual smile-lines beside his eyes were all but gone. His damp white shirt stuck to his chest, and his necktie lay on it like a long tongue. "A lot of gratitude," he said.

"Fuck that! I want a one-way bus ticket out of this dump." Katrina sat on the edge of his desk and tucked one ragged sneaker under her.

"If you want to help Mary, then do it because you care about her. Otherwise, forget it."

"I care about her," Katrina said. "I don't want her to get shipped."

"Me, neither."

Katrina jumped down off the desk, landing on the balls of her feet, already in motion toward the door. "Okay, I'm going to bring her back alive."

Downstairs, she set up her mattress, sheets, pillow, and blankets in front of the water fountain, and sat down. "They're going to ship your ass off to the nuthouse tomorrow if you don't go upstairs," she said, glancing at Mary.

Mary shrugged.

"That's what you want, isn't it?"

Mary just stared at her.

Katrina stared back. "The way I got it figured, you're doing this to get out of here," She lit a cigarette. "You got a real original way of expressing yourself. You and me, we're both original."

Mary was looking at Katrina's cigarette pack. Katrina slid it and a matchbook across the floor to her.

"I got to admire you, Mary. The way you just tune

out the whole place. I try to do that sometimes, but it only lasts for a few minutes."

Mary smiled. "I like it here," she said, lighting a cigarette.

"Hey, you're talking!" Katrina said, then saw Mary frowning. " Sorry. But let me ask you. . . . You don't have to say nothing, you can just nod or shake your head, okay? What do you mean, you like it here? You mean Fairbanks?"

Mary nodded slowly.

"Or by the water cooler here?"

Mary nodded again.

Katrina lay back on her mattress. "You really got me confused now."

"I like it here." Mary tapped the side of the water fountain.

"Oh. Okay." Katrina touched the shiny aluminum box. "Well, they probably got water fountains at the nuthouse, too."

Mary sat forward. "They don't let you sit next to them. They lock you in your room."

"Yeah?"

"The way Mr. Fox lets me stay by the water here, they wouldn't do that at the crazy hospital. And the girls come and sit with me, and even stay here at night." She smiled faintly.

"It sounds like you're sorry to be leaving."

Mary shrugged. "My father will come for me wherever I am. It don't matter."

"Yeah, I guess."

Mary leaned back and rested her head against the side of the water fountain again.

Katrina stubbed out her cigarette. "You look like you're listening to something."

Mary nodded slowly.

"You are?" Katrina sat up, holding her blanket around her. "Could I hear it, too?" When she didn't get an answer, she shifted her position until her ear was pressed against the cold metal. After a few minutes, she sat back on the mattress, rubbing her ear. "Well, I'm glad you can hear something, anyway."

Mary watched her readjust her blanket around her.

"I listen like that sometimes," Katrina said. "I stand at my window when there's a breeze and I try to feel it on my face. Then if I can, I try to, like, hear it. It's hard. I have to listen real close in between all the other noises we got all over this joint. But sometimes I can close my eyes and think about quiet places that are open and free. And I think about my grandfather. He used to take me for walks on Sunday morning when the park was empty. Sometimes it's like I can hear his voice if I listen hard enough." Katrina felt strange. She hadn't known she would say so much. "You know what I mean?" she asked.

Mary nodded. "That's why I like the water."

"Water?"

Mary pointed to the water fountain. "My people," she said.

"I don't understand."

"My people can help me." Mary wiped a tear that suddenly rolled down her cheek. "When I get thinking bad thoughts too much, my people can help me."

Katrina handed her her sheet, and Mary wiped her face on it. "I think too much, sometimes, too. What do you think about?" Katrina asked.

"Nightmares," Mary said. "I dream I'm inside a burning building and I'm looking for some way to get out."

Mary told of setting fire to her father's store. The

social workers and psychiatrists thought she had done it to hurt her father, or maybe her mother, or maybe because she was jealous of her sister. The real reason she'd done it was because she was ashamed of being poor. When she'd heard her father talking about how fire insurance worked, she knew right away how she could help the family. She set the store ablaze. But she didn't know her little sister was inside the store, and barely got her out of the fire in time. Afterwards, Mary wandered around the reservation whimpering and soaking herself with water constantly, the way the tribal doctors had soaked her sister. "The burning feeling under my skin never went away, though," Mary said. She ran her fingernails along one arm, where Katrina could see she'd been scratching a lot. "In my nightmares, the feeling turns into real flames. I can't put them out."

"Whew." Katrina touched her own arm. "Is that why you want to stay near the water fountain? "

Mary nodded, gazing far away. After a while, she looked at Katrina again, almost smiling. "You think about your grandfather. I like to think about my uncle. He tells me and my sisters stories. My favorite one's about the people who live in the water."

She leaned back against the wall. Katrina lay down to listen.

Once there was a boy named Dirty Clothes, Uncle said, who was always being teased because his clothes were ragged and old. Then one day he was nice to some tiny little people he met in the forest, and they took him on a canoe journey with them across a long pond. Uncle pointed to some leaves floating on the water—their canoes were just that size, he said. The blurred weeds under the pond's surface were the crops of the little people. At night, they would come and harvest them, but sometimes, during the day, if you looked closely, you could see them hoeing. Mary and her sisters lay down on the bank and stared at the plants and reeds and fishes. "I see one!" a sister would shout, and everyone would crowd over to her and look. Mary loved the little people, and always left pieces of bread floating on the pond for them before she left for home.

The little people made Dirty Clothes tiny like them, and gave him a suit of beautiful new clothes made out of white buckskin. When Dirty Clothes returned to his village, full grown again, he still had on the new clothes. He taught the people of his village the songs and dances that the little people had taught him. After that, Dirty Clothes was very popular in his village. If he ever felt sad or scared, he would go to the pond and talk to the little people.

Perhaps, Mary said, they would tell her how to find her way out of the fire in her nightmares. The water fountain was the place with the most water in the entire school building. "If the water in the box was spread out, it would make a small pond," she said, her dark eyes solemn as she studied it. "It feels good to be here."

Katrina, lying back on her mattress, folded her hands under her head. "Yeah. . . ."

"You ain't going to tell nobody, are you?" Mary asked suddenly.

"No, I won't tell." Katrina half-shut her eyes and imagined little people in tiny canoes sailing through the water like goldfishes. Above the ceiling, the TV was murmuring and footsteps thumped, but by concentrating on the little people, Katrina could tune out the noise. After a while, she squinted at the water fountain, hoping to see it changed in some way, maybe glowing. But it looked the same.

"There's only one thing I don't get," she said. "That fountain's not full of water. "

Mary frowned. "Yes, it is."

"No, I saw the maintenance guy repairing it one time. It's just a lot of pipes inside."

"It's water."

"In the pipes, yeah. But not unless you push the button."

"I don't believe you."

"Hey, how do you think the water gets in here? In pipes! It's no different from your own house, Mary."

Mary shook her head. "We ain't got no pipes."

"Huh? Where do you get your water from, then?"

"From the creek."

Katrina narrowed her eyes. "Okay, right. But how does it get from the creek to your house?"

"In buckets."

"What, you carry it?

"Me and my mother. Sometimes we use bottles, when we find the big plastic ones."

"Yeah, and how do you flush the damn toilet?

Mary shook her head again. "It don't use water. It's just a hole. An outhouse."

"Damn. . . ." Katrina stared at Mary's round face. "Okay. Well . . . anyway—" She reached into the pocket of her bathrobe and pulled out a dime. "The guy unscrewed the thing down here," she said, lying down to find the screw near the floor. She removed it by turning the dime in the groove. The metal side of the box opened. "Lie down. You can see the pipes under here."

Mary did. Then she scrambled to her feet. She

pounded on the top of the water fountain with both fists, spraying water, making a sound like a drum. "I thought it was full of water!" she cried, and hugged her arms across her chest. Her blanket fell to the floor. She began to make a low moaning sound that made Katrina shiver and scramble to her feet.

"I'm not saying there's no water in the pipes!" she said.

Mary turned her face to her. Her eyes were wild and damp, her cheeks puffed out. Katrina grabbed her by the lapels of her bathrobe. "I mean it! Look!" Katrina jammed her fist down onto the button and water squirted out of the aluminum hole. "It doesn't have to be full of water all the time. I mean, you probably did hear those little people anyway because—I don't know—because this is where the water comes from!"

Mary looked sideways at the water fountain, choking back tears.

"Hey, yeah," Katrina said, still holding Mary's lapels. "If you can hear them here, where there's just pipes, then you can hear them anyplace where there's pipes. Like, in the sink in your room."

Mary picked up her blanket and wrapped it around her, covering herself completely except for her face.

"You want to go up and try it in your room?" Katrina asked.

Mary looked dubiously at the staircase.

"You won't have to go to the nuthouse." Katrina squeezed Mary's arm.

Mary took a deep breath. Then she nodded. "I ain't going to tell them about what I told you."

"I won't either."

Mary stared at her for a long time. "I trust you,"

she said finally. Trailing her blanket, she headed for the stairs.

In the third-floor lounge, only the flickering glow of the television screen illuminated the faces of the girls. Wearing their bathrobes and slippers, curlers and head cloths, they sat huddled in small mounds as if facing a campfire. The air was thick with the scents of shampoo and hot-ironed hair. Occasionally, a match flared, a cigarette end glowed red, a note of quiet laughter interrupted the murmur of the television. No one noticed Mary and Katrina walk in, so Katrina slammed the door hard behind her.

Several girls turned around. "Mary!" they screamed, and everyone rushed her.

She greeted them with a scared scowl, but no one saw it in the darkness. The girls wrapped their arms around her, punched her, shoved each other to get closer to her. Mary had to sit down on the couch and cover her face with her hands.

Seeing Steven in the doorway, the girls pushed him forward. He looked stern at first, but then said, "Welcome back," and, grinning, ruffled Mary's hair. He turned to Katrina. "How'd you do it?"

Katrina shrugged.

When he had gone back into the office, the girls made room for Katrina to sit beside Mary on the couch. Getting no answers from Mary, they asked Katrina, Why was Mary sitting down there? Was she temporarily insane? How'd you talk her into coming back?

Mary smiled up at the girls' faces. Finally, Katrina waved her hands in the air, shushing everyone. "I can't say why she was downstairs and everything," she said, her voice suddenly quieter than anyone had ever heard it before. "She's got religious reasons for what she done."

The girls crowded in closer, insisting that Katrina explain. But she shook her head slowly. Her curls were loose and damp on her forehead, her face was calm. The girls backed off again, but not in anger. They looked as if they were encountering some mysterious force that was coming not only from Mary, but now from Katrina as well.

ZEROES

I picture my brother Ray walking to the mound. The dark red sun behind him bleeds across the grass of the town park. I hear a crowd in the bleachers: restless clapping, booing, the gathering thunder of feet against heavy boards. I walk up to him, removing my catcher's mask.

"A perfect pitch will win it," I say to him.

The opposing team stands along both sidelines looming like giants, their uniforms blackening in the deep twilight, the features on their faces erased by shadows. I give Ray the ball, and return to my position behind the plate.

The batter, a tall man with silver hair and a hawk nose, chops at the air as if with an axe.

Ray goes into the stretch, his leather jacket taut along his arm. I pound my fist into my mitt, making a target for him. The crowd goes silent. He'll have to aim at the sound in my mitt—the last of the sunlight has flickered out in the trees behind him.

His silhouette moves. His arm cocks back, snaps forward.

I feel a great wind approaching. A blue light expands

in the darkness, explodes in my face. The roar of a locomotive passes over me, knocking me to the ground.
But the ball is in my mitt.

* * *

During the summer when I was eleven, Ray, who was nineteen then, left boarding school. For a while, nobody knew where he was. Then he sent me a postcard which my father found in the mailbox. He called the police, and Ray was picked up two weeks later hitchhiking in Kansas.

The night he came home to Connecticut I heard an argument going on in the dining room while I ate with Mrs. Jones, the housekeeper, in her room. Afterwards, I snuck up to Ray's room with my new baseball cards.

"What was it like where you were?" I asked, sitting on his bed.

"Wide open spaces." Ray sat back in his desk chair. The military school had made him a little thinner, but it had taken most of his hair away; his head was covered with a bristly shadow.

"Can't you stay here and go to high school?"

"I'm too old. Anyway, if I stayed, I'd go nuts."

"No, you wouldn't." I squeezed my cards tight. "I wish I could go away, too," I said. I meant, with him.

He looked at the cards in my hand. "You got some new players?" he asked, smiling for the first time since he'd come home.

We spread the cards out on his rug in diamond patterns according to players' fielding positions. I badly wanted to collect a complete set of Brooklyn Dodgers—my team and his—but cards of the famous players were hard to find. I'd recently traded twenty cards for a Gil Hodges. "D'you think I got rooked?" I asked.

"No, it's a beauty." Ray lay the card down in the first baseman's position "Did you get Jackie Robinson?"

"Not yet." I grinned. I knew that if I could get Ray talking about baseball, he'd feel better, so I chattered on about Jackie Robinson. He was my favorite Dodger. I liked to hear Red Barber, the radio announcer, talk about the way he teased pitchers as he led off base. Base stealing was the part of the game I liked best. You could do something all on your own that was normally not allowed, but if you got away with it, everyone cheered instead of getting mad at you. I got in fights at day camp about who was the better player, Jackie or the Yankee's Joe DiMaggio. The camp, which was mostly for stuck-up Country Day School boys, was lousy with Yankee fans. It puzzled me that Ray, though a devout Dodger fan, also thought there were things to be said for Joe or Ted Williams or Stan Musial. He always wanted to be fair to everyone.

"Jackie had to wait till he was twenty-nine to play in the majors, just because he was a Negro!" I explained.

"Does that make him a better player?" Then Ray answered his question. "Yes, in the long run, it probably does."

The next night, I ate in the dining room with my parents and Ray. No one said much—the echoes of the previous night's shouting still hung like shadows in the corners. After desert, my father sat tall in his chair and combed his silver hair back from his forehead with his fingers. "Well, Ray," he said. "What are you going to do with your life now, if you don't mind me asking?"

Ray looked down at his plate. "I'm thinking," he said, his voice quiet and slow, "of joining the service."

"Wonderful," my father said. "The son of the head waiter at the club is going into the army. We'll have lots to talk about, won't we?"

Ray looked up slowly, focusing on the candle flame between him and my father. "I hate your sarcasm." He said in a low, quiet voice that seemed to make his back teeth vibrate. "I hate the way it makes me panic, so I can never do anything but hang my damn head."

My father's mouth fell open. I gripped the edge of the table, looking from face to face, feeling both terrified and exultant. My mother's ice cubes clinked in her glass as she raised it from the table.

"Anyway, this should make you happy. . . ." Ray broke the silence. "I'm thinking of joining the Air Force."

My father's adam's apple rose in his throat. "Oh. I see. Well, that's. . . ." He swallowed. "We ought to talk about this, Ray."

After dinner they went up to my father's room. Passing the open door, I saw them sitting on the bed with one of my father's big World War I aviation books open on their knees.

I told Mrs. Jones about this. Having heard on the radio that a war against the communists was going on in Korea, I worried that Ray might get shot down there. "A sensitive boy like Ray's the kind the Air Force will keep on the ground, if they keep him at all," she said.

Ray enlisted. On the night before he was to leave, my mother cooked him a steak dinner. My father seemed a lot more cheerful about Ray's decision than Ray was. I watched him chewing grimly as if with exposed nerve-ends instead of teeth.

"How are you going to spend your last day as a civilian, son?" My father wiped his mouth; a smile remained when he removed the napkin. "I can reserve us a court at the club tomorrow."

"I want to see the Dodgers play one last time," Ray said, and turned to me. "Want to come?"

"Yes!" I said before my father could object.

* * *

The train looked new, the sides of its cars gleaming silver as if illuminated from within. The windows reflected light like a row of mirrors. As soon as we pulled out of the Ridge Haven station, Ray yanked off his necktie and let out a long breath. "Erskine's on the mound today," he said, opening his newspaper.

I'd been staring out the window at a shelf of fat dark rain clouds hovering above the telephone poles, but said nothing about them. "Is Erskine still your favorite pitcher?"

"Mmm." He said, studying the paper. "But he hasn't been having a great year."

I had several Carl Erskine cards; they weren't hard to get. He had a sad, open face, like the man who ran the Gulf station in town. "What's he—about four and five this season?" I asked. Ray nodded. I twisted in the seat until I could see behind the paper. "What's that?" I asked, pointing to the page.

"Just a box score."

I wished he would explain what the letters and numbers meant, but his gaze was sunk so deeply into the newsprint that I didn't want to disturb him. Once he said, "It's probably dumb, going into the city now when I have to come back tonight." He meant to the recruiting station, where another train would take him to a camp down South.

"It's not dumb," I said.

I loved being on the train—the clicking of the wheels beneath me, the long plume of sound the locomotive gave off when we went around the curves—but Brooklyn was even better. The streets crowded with of people of all different skin colors, the bluesy music blasting from record stores, the swarthy old men talking in barber shop doorways, the sudden strange spicy food smells we walked through—everything made me stare, take deep breaths, stop and listen with my head cocked. The more foreign it was, the better I liked it.

As I rounded a corner, Ebbets Field appeared before me like the prow of a huge old freighter washed up onto the asphalt. The place gave off a faint roar that vibrated just above my head. I sensed another universe behind those walls, where gods roamed hidden from view; I heard the crack of a bat echo deep inside the place, and shivered. The afternoon was unusually dark and damp; massive banks of lights over the stadium flashed on all at once; I stopped in my tracks as the glow floated like a cloud of silver steam above the walls.

At a souvenir stand, Ray bought a blue cap with a gothic white B above the bill. "This is the official Dodger cap." He handed it to me.

"Hey, thanks!" I ran my finger slowly over the felt crown. "Aren't you going to get one, too?" I asked.

"The government's going to give me a cap tonight," he said.

"Wait!" I handed the vendor a crumpled dollar from my back pocket and grabbed another blue cap. "Here!" I thrust it into Ray's hands.

"Well, okay." He put it on. I was glad to see his bristly hair disappear beneath it. "For good luck," he said. "I'll need it."

I'd only seen black and white pictures of the stadium, and was started to see that the playing field was in color. Under hundreds of artificial suns, the grass glowed green as if each blade had just been washed. The bases were white as big vanilla cakes. An old man dusted off our seats with a huge mitten and Ray gave him a quarter, though the seats hadn't needed cleaning. My brother obviously knew that this was part of going to a ball game. He bought hot dogs for us, a beer and a cigar for himself, a Coke and peanuts for me. The hot dog squirted salty juice into my mouth; the Coke—forbidden at home because of the dangerous drugs it contained—made a fizzy laughing sound in my paper cup. The aroma of Ray's cigar smoke lingered around us.

The seats filled during batting practice. Men called out to the players by their first names as if they knew them personally. These weren't Dodgers, they were Giants, but they were baseball players, the first live ones I'd ever seen. The field became a blur of balls being thrown around and smacked into leather gloves. My eyes ached from trying to watch everything at once.

"This is almost the best part," Ray said as a batter hit one lofting fly ball after another. "Nobody has to win or loose. They're just doing what they love to do."

He pointed out various Giants by name. Most I'd only vaguely heard of, players whose cards I'd traded away to get Dodgers. One Giant's name was familiar: Elmer Vlacek. His card said he was the only major league player born in Europe—in Czechoslovakia, which I knew was behind the Iron Curtain. Watching him, I figured that it must have been be hard to grow up in a communist country where kids probably weren't allowed to play baseball. Elmer had a round face with one cheek puffed out from chewing tobacco just like any American ballplayer. He didn't look like a communist to me. I couldn't see the point of going to war to shoot people like him.

Kids in dirty shirts and jeans were hanging over the rail of the box seats below us, reaching for stray baseballs. One kid leaned so far over he fell onto the grass. Retrieving a ball, he scrambled back into the stands. A guard came running and grabbed him by the collar.

"*Booo!*" Ray shouted. I'd never heard him raise his voice to anyone before. Several other fans booed the guard, too. The guard let the kid go, but snatched the ball out of his hand and tossed it back onto the field. I booed loudly.

Then an amazing thing happened. Elmer Vlacek walked over, picked up the ball, and tossed it to the boy. He caught it, letting out a whoop. Ray laughed. I hoped Elmer would get lots of hits today.

"I sort of don't want the game to start," Ray said. "Once it starts, it's partly over." He looked at the ash on his cigar. "There's no big leagues where I'm going."

"Mrs. Jones said you won't have to fly planes in Korea," I said.

"I'm only going to Alabama tonight. Boot camp. It'll be full of crackers there. You know what they are?"

I shook my head.

"They're the kind of people who called Jackie Robinson 'nigger' when he first came up to the majors. They don't like Northern boys much, either." Suddenly he turned toward the field. "Hey, there's our Dodgers."

Now the field was alive with players in baggy blue and white uniforms. Dust clouds rose from under their cleats as they ran. I didn't need to look at the scorecard to recognize them. Gil Hodges had big ears, like his picture on my baseball card. Pee Wee Reese really was smaller than the others. When Jackie Robinson ran out to second base, he didn't deign to notice the boos mixed with the cheers. I watched him field grounders, sweeping his glove along the ground as if he were scooping up stationary turnips instead of fast-moving baseballs. Nothing got by him. He threw so fast to first base that the ball disappeared in the air until it exploded into Hodges' mitt. Over the stadium I could see the heavy clouds squatting on the roof, but the banks of lights gave the place a radiance of its own.

"Ladies and gentlemen," the public address voice boomed, "Miss Gladys Gooding will now play our national anthem." Organ music filled the stadium. I hummed along.

The first batter walked toward the plate. But now thin diagonal lines of rain were filling the space under the lights. The air smelled wet. Ray kept looking up at the sky. The drops of moisture against his face made him wince continually. It was first time I'd seen his tic since we'd gotten on the train.

No one got any hits during the first three innings. Jackie Robinson didn't get on, so he couldn't steal any bases. Elmer Vlacek wasn't playing; maybe he was being punished for giving the kid the ball.

"I like games where there's lots of hitting and scoring," Ray said. "I wouldn't care who won if they started doing *something*."

"It's a pitcher's duel," I said. That's what Red Barber called games like this on the radio. "Maybe it'll be a no-hitter."

Ray shook his head. "They only happen once or twice a season. The odds against them are millions to one."

"Still—"

"You ask for too much, you get nothing at all," he said, his voice startlingly sharp. When he saw my face, his eyes started blinking furiously. "Forget that, okay? I'm just wound up today. You want some more peanuts?"

"Okay," I said, and he waved the peanut vendor over. The first peanuts were hard to open; my fingers didn't work well.

Carl Furillo struck out. He had the highest average in the league; if he couldn't get a hit, what chance did the Dodgers have? I had to go to the bathroom. It wasn't easy to find in the echoing cement caverns under the stands; the urinals were overflowing and stank of sour beer foam. When I came back, the field didn't seem green any more; it was a dark, soaked gray. The players standing in their positions looked bored, waiting for something to happen. It occurred to me that a lot of baseball consisted of waiting around. Grey boredom and rain got into the park whether people booed or cheered. Looking down from the ramp at my brother hunched in his seat under the drizzle, I could see that he was just hanging around, too. I suddenly saw my own life as a lot of time spent waiting for nothing very terrific to happen. Like Ray, I couldn't do much about this. Maybe nobody could, not even baseball players.

I sat down again. "You okay?" I asked Ray.

"Sure." He sat up straight. "We got a run—look."

The scoreborard showed the Dodgers ahead one to nothing.

"A double, an error, and a fielder's choice. You didn't miss much." Ray was trying to sound cheerful. "Look who's coming up."

The big man with the deep black face strode toward the batter's box. Then he stopped. I leaned forward. Two umpires were talking to each other near the pitcher's mound. Jackie Robinson walked away from the plate. The rain had begun to pelt down.

The fielders ran into their dugout. Groundskeepers rolled a huge tarpaulin onto the infield, turning it into an instant lake with raindrops bouncing like B-B's on its shiny surface. Behind us, people were taking shelter under the overhanging roof, but Ray just sat where he was with his knees drawn up, staring out at the slanting lines of rain.

"You go ahead," he said, his shoulders drooping. "I just feel like sitting here."

"Me, too." I pulled the bill of my cap down.

Ray didn't speak for a long time. Now and then he chewed his nails, something my father always got after him about. The rain hissed faintly like air slowly leaving a balloon. The faraway bleachers began to fade into a mist.

"The game doesn't count if it doesn't go five innings," he said. Rain was trickling down his cheeks.

"It does, too!" I said.

He looked at his cigar. It had gone out.

I decided that I wanted to be the last person to leave the stadium if they cancelled the game; I'd rather be here with Ray watching the raindrops splashing in Brooklyn than be anyplace else in the sunshine.

After half an hour, the rain finally let up, though the dark clouds continued to lie low over the roof. The tarpaulin was rolled away. As the players ran back into the outfield, their cleats made splashes on the grass. I was soaked but didn't mind; the air was warm. With all my might I pictured players hitting doubles, triples, home runs that would make Ray jump up and down and cheer.

Jackie Robinson, returning to the plate, grounded out. Batter after batter grounded out, struck out, flied out. A few Dodgers got hits but were left on base. The zeros kept appearing on the scoreboard like blank mocking cartoon eyes.

Giants　　0 0 0 0 0 　　R 0　　H 0
Dodgers　0 0 0 1 0 0　　R 1　　H 3

Suddenly I turned to Ray, who was staring at the field as if he were already watching out the window of a train heading south to Alabama. "Hey, the Giants still haven't got any hits," I said. "Isn't that a no-hitter?"

He sat up. "Listen," he said. "There's three innings left."

"Okay, okay," I said, but I could tell by the way Ray concentrated on Carl Erskine as he warmed up on the mound that he was thinking about a no-hitter, too. Carl still looked like the gas station manager. When he took off his cap to wipe his forehead— the drizzle had started again—I saw that he was partly bald. I never knew players could be bald under their caps. Beside wiry Pee Wee Reese and huge dark Jackie Robinson and Gil Hodges standing like a mountain over first base, Carl looked very ordinary. He didn't throw the ball too hard, and everyone hit it somewhere. But not for a base hit.

"Only two innings more." I said, as the seventh 0 went up on the scoreboard. "And it'll be a no-hitter, right?"

"*Shhh!*"

"Why?"

"You're not supposed to say it. It's sort of like magic. Saying the words out loud might keep it from happening." Ray squeezed his empty beer cup.

"So if we keep it a secret, we could help...." I shut my mouth.

"Maybe," Ray said. "That's the idea, anyway."

I noticed that the people around us seemed keyed up, as if they were all sharing a powerful secret. An old guy who'd looked like a bum was grinning and waving his arm in the air with every pitch; he didn't look like a bum now. The kid who'd picked up the ball during batting practice leaned over the front of the box seats with all his friends; the guard saw them, but didn't chase them away. He was watching the field.

Carl Erskine came up to bat and struck out on three pitches. "He's saving his strength," I said. Ray agreed. The people around us must have understood this as well—they clapped for Erskine as he walked back to the dugout. When the first Giant in the eighth inning grounded out, I could feel in my seat the vibrations of thousands of feet stomping.

"Attaboy, Erskine!" the old man shouted. "Humbaby!" The kids at the box seats' rail jumped up and down. The stadium rocked with cheers, the huge freighter shifting on moving waters. Then, as the next Giant stood waiting at the plate, the crowd hushed, as if a wind had died down suddenly. The world stayed precariously level. Then: a pop-up. The stadium rocked and trembled again. Grown men were jumping to their feet and yelling at the top of their lungs like kids. I'd never seen men in Ridge Haven behave that way.

"Get outa there, ya jerk!" Someone shouted at the next batter. No one even glanced at him.

I jumped up. "Get out!" I screamed. "Beat it!"

I looked down at my brother to see if my noisiness bothered him. He was never rude to people. But he just grinned up at me.

The Giant hit a line drive over third base. I covered my eyes. The crowd made a loud "*Ohhhh!*" sound that moved like a wave along the stands.

"It's just a foul ball," Ray said, nudging me.

"Whew." I dropped my hands from my face and stood on my seat.

Another pitch: the batter swung and missed. "Strike Three!" the umpire yelled. The storm exploded again.

All the people in front of us were standing now, blocking Ray's view. "Don't you want to see?" I shouted at him.

He slid down in his seat. "Your turn—you tell me what's happening."

"Okay." The batter took a third strike. "He's out!" I screamed to Ray over the roar of the crowd. "The inning's over!"

Ray gave me the high sign, his forefinger and thumb meeting to make an *0*.

Everyone sat down while Brooklyn batted. We

were just waiting for Carl Erskine to take the mound again. It wasn't like waiting for rain to stop. I sensed a new feeling in the air: people thinking that all the magic they were trying to work—by not saying the words "no-hitter"—might actually make it happen. All around me, strangers were grinning at each other and talking in hushed voices. Ray re-lit his cigar and sat back, the smoke rising from it like a tiny banner unfurling.

I knew I shouldn't say anything, but I couldn't keep still, and leaned close to whisper to Ray. "You think—maybe. . . ?"

His whole face seemed to be struggling to speak. Finally he rested his hand on my head for a moment. Under the circumstances, it didn't seem like an awkward gesture.

Now Carl Erskine's methodical warm-up pitches were the most fascinating thing going on anywhere. People cheered every time he threw, even though there was no batter yet. I kept rolling my eyes along all the zeros on the top line of the scoreboard.

Giants	0 0 0 0 0 0 0	R 0	H 0
Dodgers	0 0 0 1 0 0 0 1	R 2	H 6

The first batter of the ninth inning chopped his bat beside the plate, glaring at the pitcher, aiming invisible line drives past his head. Carl's shoulders drooped. He looked tired and vulnerable. The gray outfield seemed vast behind him and the high walls of the stadium loomed out of the drizzle. Was he scared? I was. If he messed up, and if something bad happened to Ray in Korea—I remembered crashing planes to the floor in the war games we'd played in the attic, years before—then I'd look back and think, it all started with that day we went to Brooklyn. Ray hadn't asked for anything as risky as a might-be no-hitter, he'd just wanted to see a ball game. Why did this dumb pitcher have to try to bring off something so impossible?

Then Pee Wee and Gil and Jackie all leaned forward around the infield, poised to spring to Carl's defense. The clapping and stamping and cheering from the stands died down a little. Carl straightened up. Suddenly he didn't look so hesitant and ordinary any more. He threw a ball, a strike, and then the batter hit a grounder to shortstop. Pee Wee threw to Gil, and everyone jumped up to scream. Ray got to his feet. I started to shout insults at the next batter stepping out from the Giants dugout. But then I shut my mouth, feeling queasy.

"What's the matter?" Ray asked.

"It's Elmer Vlacek. He's pinch-hitting." For an awful moment, I had the impulse to shoot him down in cold blood at the plate.

"Oh." Ray winced at the boos starting up around us. "Well, if he gets a hit, he'll be a hero. If he doesn't, Erskine will be. Either way, it's pretty good, huh?"

I stared at Ray. Could he really be so cheerful? Not judging by the look on his face. His mouth was stretched in a grimace, his eyes narrowed. I could tell he needed this no-hitter even more than I did.

"I don't want to watch," I said, sitting down hard.

"Okay. . . . Strike one," he called down to me. Then he pulled me by the arm. "Come on, I need you here with me!"

I leapt to my feet. Standing on the seat, I leaned against Ray's shoulder. He clamped his cigar between his teeth.

I saw Elmer's body jerk around. His bat made a

cracking sound that hit me between the eyes. A groan went up all around me. The ball went screaming into the hole between shortstop and second.

Suddenly Jackie Robinson sprawled onto the grass, one arm trapped under him, the other stretched straight out. The stadium rocked with noise. He had the ball in his glove. He'd caught it for an out!

Pee Wee ran over to him. Jackie stood up slowly, holding his stomach. His head down, he walked in a circle, brushed off his uniform. Then he crouched behind second base again. The roar of the crowd surged out of the grandstands.

I knew that the next batter didn't stand a chance. Ray was leaning sideways against me now. He seemed to know it, too. Carl was throwing hard, his arm snapping forward as he zinged the ball toward the plate. Strike one—pop! Into the catcher's glove. Then a ball. Then a hard pitch, a perfect one right down the middle . . . and tap! A soft one-hopper bounced back to the mound. Carl grabbed it as if snatching a gnat out of the air. He turned and tossed a sure, slow strike to first base.

He had his no-hitter!

Suddenly I was caught up in a huge screaming mob. I stood on my seat and yelled as the players rushed to Carl and hugged him and smacked him on the back. They all ran together toward the dugout, heads up, grinning. Fans swarmed onto the field. Even as the stadium emptied, I kept screaming until my voice gave out altogether. I hadn't realized it, but I was clutching Ray's arm, my fingers digging into his shirt. I tried to say something to him, but only a scratchy sound came out of my mouth. He looked dazed, his mouth half open, his eyes fixed on the dugout where all the Dodgers had disappeared. When I shook him, a wobbly smile appeared on his face.

I would have been crushed on the throbbing stairs under the stands if Ray hadn't kept his arm tight around my shoulder. People were pressed up against me on all sides; all I saw was sweat-soaked backs of shirts until we were suddenly squeezed out into the daylight. The rows of brick tenements, the overhead wires, the gray cheesecloth clouds overhead—everything vibrated before my eyes.

I wanted to watch until the very last of the fans poured out of the stadium, and all the vendors rolled away their pushcarts. I wanted to stay in Brooklyn forever. Ray was in no hurry to leave, either. He wandered around with me, gazing at the people as if they were old friends. Finally he bought two scorecards and two official Brooklyn Dodger pencils.

As the subway train roared through the tunnel, I stood tight against my brother's side in the mob, swaying with him into the turns, feeling the train rumble around me like an echo of Ebbets Field's pandemonium. I could picture the stadium somewhere above me, the huge freighter still rocking, sailing away into a gauzy sky on raucous waves of applause.

At Grand Central Station, my face ached from grinning all the way from Brooklyn. Men in suits were racing for commuter trains as if this were an ordinary afternoon. The evening papers weren't out yet, so no one here but us knew that Carl Erskine had just thrown a no-hitter. At the very moment this occurred to me, Ray turned to me and said, "They don't realize, do they?"

"I know!"

He gave my cap's bill a tug. Then he stared up at

the big clock over the entrance to the tracks. It was time to catch the train to Ridge Haven.

When we'd found a seat, I hoped the train would break down on the way home. Then Ray took out the scorecards he'd bought and handed me one. "You've got to help me with the box score."

He showed me how to fill in the little squares with letters and numbers that recorded what each batter had done, inning by inning. I remembered plays for him and copied his notations with my Brooklyn Dodgers pencil. It seemed important to finish filling in the squares before we reached our station. We had it all done except for Elmer Vlacek's at-bat in the ninth inning. Ray chewed on the pencil's eraser. How could he have forgotten Jackie Robinson's diving catch? I reminded him, and he wrote it in, nodding.

"Now, watch this," he said, moving the pencil point. He wrote nine *0*'s in a row after "Giants." Then he drew a final round *0* under the total of hits. "Look at all those perfect zeros." He grinned.

I filled in the *0*'s on my own scorecard and carefully rolled it up around my pencil. So as not to make the pencil shorter by sharpening it, I decided never to write anything else with it again.

Trees and buildings flicked by outside the glass. Ray sat beside the window, the scorecard resting on his knee. His eyes were shut, all twitching subsided. I sat in exactly the same position beside him, except my eyes were wide open. Rain streaked down outside the train now, splattering the window. But those banks of suns over Ebbets field—those banks of perfect incandescent zeros—gave us a glow, and I felt it radiating all around my face. Ray and I were the only ones who could see it.

The aura moved with us as we climbed down off the train and got into my mother's car. Its interior was lit up by our grins, and my mother, seeing them, began to smile a little. Ray told her how Jackie Robinson saved the day with his diving catch, and I wanted to tell her about Ray's player, the spectacular Carl Erskine—but he gave me a glance and I knew I mustn't tell anyone, not yet. No-hitter magic was still on; saying the word might make us go out like a couple of light bulbs. We kept them lit.

I watched Ray and my mother standing at the counter in the pantry while he poured gin over some ice cubes. Usually he didn't say much to her unless she asked him questions, but tonight they were chatting quietly as they had a drink together. It occurred to me that Ray was very much a grown-up now and had been for some time. I liked watching the two of them leaning back against the counter with glasses in their hands. I couldn't hear what they were saying, but now and then Mother made a laughing sound; she was inside the bulb of light with us now.

Then she heard my father's car on the driveway and finished her drink in a gulp.

Ray and I and Mother stayed inside our incandescent aura all through dinner. We saw my father's remarks spatter on the glass, but they didn't reach us. When he started to tell Ray about how tennis was a better sport than baseball because you could keep playing it all your life and it helped you to make friends and business contacts, Ray looked at me and we smiled, knowing better.

My father had a going-away present for Ray: a leather manicure kit with a red silk lining. Inside, tight leather loops held in place odd-shaped clippers and tweezers. They looked to me like strapped-down silver insects. Ray and I had seen these kits in the window of an expensive gift shop in Grand Central Station; my father must have bought the gift there while rushing to catch his train. I could see that Ray was disappointed with it, almost angry, and suddenly the glass bulb seemed about to crack. But he reached out and took the leather kit from my father. He said, "Thank you" in a quiet voice, and glanced at me.

Mother said Ray would be the only one in boot camp with anything so fancy. My father shot her a look that sliced through the air like a back-hand swipe, but she half-shut her eyes and it was deflected by invisible glass.

Finally my father began talking about his World War I Air Corps boot camp, where he learned to fly planes made of wood and canvas and wire. Ray and I glanced at each other; I pictured the combat game we'd played on the attic floor: the pilot rescuing the bombardier from the burning plane. Gradually Dad's voice penetrated our incandescence. It shone too: a web of crackling white wires reflecting in the glossy dark surface of the table. Even Mother appeared to like listening to Dad's old stories. A glow surrounded the table, with all of us sheltering together inside it, as talk of warfare brought a rare peace to the family.

Later that night, we drove through the rain to the train station. Ray stood awkwardly on the platform with his duffel bag. He wore his baseball cap to kept the rain from falling onto his face. We all waited as silence dropped off the roof around us.

The train pulled in, its brakes scraping beneath its belly. Ray kissed my mother and shook my father's hand. Then he hugged me good-bye. I dug my fingers into his leather jacket, my eyes stinging. He gave the bill of my Dodgers cap a tug.

"We were there," I whispered.

He made the sign with his thumb and forefinger shaped like an *0*. Then, swinging his duffel ahead of him, he climbed the steps into the train. The car's door swung open. He vanished through it.

The train looked grimy in the weak station light. Slowly, jerkily, it started to gather speed. I smelled acrid steam. Up ahead, the locomotive gave off a rhythmic chuffing sound.

Breaking free of my parents, I raced down the station platform, yelling and waving wildly at the windows. The train's whistle carried my voice off into the night.

THE EDUCATED BILLY-GOATS

The children ran away, shrieking. They dashed into the huts to alert their mothers, then ran outside again, heedless of their mothers' warnings. Some crouched behind granaries, their faces pressed into the miniature thatched roofs. Others climbed up the pole fences of the cattle-pen. There, concealed behind fans of banana leaves, they could watch the strangers from a safe distance. Their whispering blended with the buzz of flies and the slow shifting sound the leaves made in the breeze.

The tall white man stopped in an open space in the center of the compound. His parade of green-uniformed schoolboys halted behind him. The children were suddenly as still as huts and granaries and fence posts.

The teacher wiped the sweat from his eyes. Open doorways of huts stared back at him, dark rectangles of shadows. He noted signs of life in the compound—a maize cob lying abandoned on its stone mortar, a dress hanging in a window, still dripping from a recent washing. Footprints were everywhere, and the scent of dust seemed freshly made by scurrying feet. But there was no one in sight.

"What should we do now?" His voice sounded loud in the silence.

Peter Wanjala, the Bukusu boy that Lockery had chosen as the group's interpreter, glanced around uncomfortably. He wished he had never heard of oral history field trips. He caught sight of a shirtless boy chasing a cow across a field, and wished he could be fleeing into the underbrush with him. "We can just wait, Sir. Someone will come," he said.

"I think we should go away," Pius Otieno said.

The two Baganda boys crowded close behind Otieno. Ordinarily, they had no use for this small, cheeky Luo, but he had just expressed their feelings exactly. They were not happy about being chosen for this field trip, either. Throughout history, their kings, the monarchs of the great Buganda empire, had made serfs of placid tribes like these Babukusu who lived near the school. What could possibly be interesting about learning the history of serfs? The boys watched their teacher's face for some flicker of uncertainty, a gap between his resolve and his present predicament into which they might drive a wedge.

"No, we won't go away just yet," Lockery said. He wiped his face again and looked around hopefully. "Someone'll come soon." He glanced at Wanjala, but Wanjala looked away.

"Perhaps we try another farm," Otieno insisted.

"No, this is the one we want. Elija is the biggest man around here. We get his support, we'll get all the people's support." Lockery had done an undergraduate minor in anthropology; he knew that to get information about people, you always went to the headman first. "Then we'll be able to go on lots more field trips," he added.

"It is very hot in the sun." Mwanga, a Muganda, touched the top of his head. "These people are very rude, not to come out and greet us."

"I'm the one that's got to worry about sunburn, not you," Lockery laughed. "Go sit in the shade, if you're hot."

But no one moved. Without the teacher the boys had no acceptable reason for being here. They didn't want to be separated from him, even by a few paces.

"You're looking nervous, Sir," Otieno, said. "Why do you want to stay?"

Lockery shrugged. "I'm always nervous. It's my nature." His eyes followed the wavy lines that the conical thatched rooftops made against the sky. They were a soft yellow-brown color, and the sky was bright blue behind them. "No, I'll tell you what it is, Otieno," he said. "I love new situations. Places that are utterly foreign to me. I get excited when I'm about to learn something I knew absolutely nothing about before." He smiled. "Can you understand that?"

Otieno grinned and shook his head. He liked Mr. Lockery because he would talk about himself as if he were not a Sir, as if his students were not students but just people. "I don't understand," Otieno said.

"Excuse me, Sir," Mwanga was holding the top of his head again. "It is very hot here."

"Yeah, okay, Mwanga. We'll go find some shade." Lockery led the four boys to a shady spot under an overhanging roof. He took out his packet of Crown Birds. "Go ahead. We're off school grounds," he said, offering the packet around. Everyone took a cigarette but Wanjala, the Bukusu. He didn't want his own people to see him with a cigarette. They would think him pretentious, smoking like a European or a town rogue. He was embarrassed enough, waiting here like a beggar, uninvited and unannounced, and keeping company with a gang of arrogant royalists.

The two Baganda students began to speak Luganda in low voices. "Henry Morton Stanley, the great explorer, was kind to his native bearers," Mwanga said, sounding like the history textbook. "He won the Africans' devotion by giving out cigarettes."

"And showed his humility by lighting them for the Africans with his own match," Ssanango added.

"Yes. He made a fire with a tiny stick. A wondrous invention from across the great waters. The natives thought him to be a god." Mwanga took a long drag on his cigarette and wrinkled his nose. He was used to filter-tips. "But his true colors were shown when all the natives died poisoned from his Cheap Bird cigarettes."

Ssanango was holding his cigarette like a fountain pen. He made a face, too, though he didn't know one brand of cigarettes from another. He had some catching up to do. "I think his bar-maid friend's mattress must be covered with tobacco crumbs every morning, after he has pedaled his bicycle away," he said.

Mwanga grinned. "She has to sweep them out of her pussy with a broom." He bit his knuckles to keep from laughing.

Lockery frowned at them and the two boys kept silent. He didn't, of course, know Luganda.

Wanjala tensed. He heard approaching footsteps.

"What do you want me to say, Mr. Lockery?"

"You remember—what we talked about in class."

"I remember some things you were saying. But I am forgetting too much."

"All right. You introduce us first. Then you say we're interested in finding out about the way things used to be here. The way things were before Europeans and other tribes came, before there were shops and motorcars and schools. We want to talk to the old people, so that we can learn from them."

Wanjala opened his mouth. He wanted more prepping. But it was too late.

A woman hobbled out into the courtyard, her eyes lowered to avoid the stares of the strangers. Her breasts dangled visibly beneath her faded dress as she came forward. She was not old; her hobbling was caused by a club foot. The toes of one foot were pointing backwards. Wanjala's heart sank. That a mere woman should have been sent to greet the visitors was a bad enough sign. But this woman—he knew of her—was a cripple; she was Elija's only barren wife, the outcast among the other wives. "Mirembe," he greeted her, as politely as he could manage.

The woman shook his hand, her eyes still lowered. "Mirembe."

Wanjala repeated what the teacher had told him, almost an exact translation. Then he added some words of praise for Elija, the head of the homestead, and offered apologies for disturbing him.

The woman said that Elija was not at home, She glanced behind her. Muffled voices were coming from the hut she had just left. She repeated what she had said in a quavering voice.

"The woman says that Elija is not present, Sir," Wanjala said.

"Ask her if there's someone else we could talk to."

Wanjala took a deep breath. He continued his greeting, praising Elija's livestock and the abundance of his fields. As he spoke, he glanced at the hut where the muffled voices were growing louder. The woman balanced herself on her one good foot by holding her hands out from her sides. She kept upsetting her balance by trying to cover the worn places in her dress where dusty brown skin showed through. Wanjala glanced at her and at the hut, and decided not to ask the teacher's question.

"The woman says there is no one else here to talk to," he reported.

"I didn't hear her say anything, Wanjala—"

The commotion in the hut burst outside. A man appeared in the doorway, thrashing his arms. A woman scrambled out in front of him. She tried to push him back inside, but he flung her from him. She fell against the wall of the hut with a wail. The children who had been tugging at the man's pantlegs scattered.

The man lurched forward, waving a heavy, twisted walking-stick in the air, His shirt was buttoned awry, showing his stomach, but he did not look foolish. His hair was white and his eyes glowed with red veins. His stride, though unsteady, was the stride of a man used to having people jump out of his way. He came to a halt in front of Wanjala and waved his stick in the air. What, he demanded, were these strangers doing on his land?

Wanjala stumbled backwards. The walking-stick had passed dangerously close to his face, and the man's breath was a powerful stench. Wanjala started to explain why he was here, but the man cut him off, roaring. When he finally closed his mouth, he planted the stick firmly at his feet. The stick said : You approach no closer than this.

"What's the matter, Wanjala?" Lockery asked.

"He is very drunken, Sir." Wanjala took another step backwards. "He is saying many nonsenses."

"Is he Elija, himself?"

"Yes, he is," Wanjala said. "We should go, Sir."

Lockery wanted to step back, too, but he didn't. "What's he saying, Wanjala?"

"He says I have cost him the bride-wealth for his daughter. But it was not me, Sir. I swear it by the Holy Ghost!"

"What are you talking about?"

"He has mistaken me for another Bukusu boy. This boy is in form four. He made one of Elija's daughters to be with child. Now Elija cannot get bride-wealth for her. It will be difficult to find any good husband for her, he is saying. He wants a fine to be paid for his daughter's child. He will kill the boy who is responsible, if he does not get it." Wanjala wiped his face with both hands. "Elija is angry, Sir," he added.

The old man lifted his stick and shouted several rapid sentences. His voice was as deep as a man twice his size and weight,

"He is also angry because there are Buganda boys here. He does not like Bugandas."

Mwanga and Ssanango had been grinning at each other, but their faces suddenly became very sober.

The old man leaned forward, reached out his hand, and clutched Wanjala's shoulder as if the boy were a mere rabbit. A woman wailed. Children gasped, a mass intake of breath from all sides. They were suddenly visible, totem-poles of small brown faces peering round the corners of huts, Wanjala shut his eyes tight. He expected a blow from the stick at any second. But Elija only shook him hard by his shirt and pointed the stick at the teacher. He roared and belched, roared and waved his stick in the direction of the school. The bristly beard beneath the corners of his mouth was shiny with saliva. He gripped Wanjala's shoulder tighter.

"He says the school is responsible," Wanjala whimpered. His eyes were clamped shut. "He says teachers should be in their classrooms teaching. They should not be roving about the countryside to bother the honest farmers." This, in fact, was a loose translation. Elija's diatribe had been about teachers who let their schoolboys run wild, destroying the morals of the local girls, and failing to show proper respect for their elders.

Lockery clenched his fists to keep his hands from trembling. "Tell him we're sorry we've bothered him. Tell him also—Wanjala listen—" Wanjala tried to twist his face away. "Tell him I'm going to speak to the headmaster of the school. The headmaster will make the boy pay the fine for the daughter's baby."

"But the headmaster, he does not know which boy it is."

"No, but you do."

"I can't tell."

"All right, but then Elija's going to think it's you."

"It's not, Sir!"

"How do I know it's not? Elija's pointed at you."

"It is only because I am from the school."

Lockery said nothing.

"If I tell him, he will hear. He will send his sons to beat the boy."

"Well, what's his Christian name?"
"William."
"Whose class is he in first period?"
"Mr. Stuart's." Wanjala opened his eyes. "Make him let me go, Sir!"
"Tell him I know who the boy is. I'll tell the headmaster, and Elija will get his fine."
Wanjala's voice cracked as he spoke. But Elija's grip on him remained firm. He wiped his mouth and spoke in a low voice, his jaw protruding.
"He will not let me go unless I tell him the boy's name now," Wanjala said.
The teacher glared at the old man. For a moment, their eyes were locked. "He will never know the boy's name or get his fine," Lockery said slowly, "unless he lets you go right now. And unless he agrees to talk with us."
Wanjala spoke. Elija turned back toward the teacher. His jaw was still thrust out stubbornly, but there was a trace of a sly smile in his eyes. Lockery smiled back briefly, then waited.
Elija shoved Wanjala away from him.
Another gasping sound came from all sides. The huts themselves seemed to have been holding their breaths and swelling, but now were settling back to normal size. A woman wailed; it was a happy-sounding wail this time. The crippled woman stopped shielding her eyes from Elija—the explosion was over.
A woman in a phosphorescent yellow dress ran up to Elija. He grunted and tried to step away, but she moved closer to him. She smiled and touched his cheek. Her voice was high and soothing. As she moved, her yellow dress billowed out about her ankles, reflecting the sunlight's glare with a brilliance that was surprising, among these earth-colored huts.

The old man continued to protest to the woman, but now and then he smiled, too, as if the sun itself had rolled into his courtyard to bathe him in its rays.

The woman held Elija's arm and spoke to Lockery in Bukusu.

"She is apologizing for the behavior of her husband," Wanjala said. "He was celebrating the birth of a son when we came. He was drinking much beer."

The teacher nodded. He smiled at the woman and at Elija. "Are you all right, Wanjala?"

"No, Sir. It is giving me much anguish." Wanjala rubbed his shoulder, a neutral spot of pain between his resentment toward his teacher and his anger at Elija for shaming him before his teacher. "My people, they are not like Elija. They are not drunkards," Wanjala said, his voice cracking again. "It is very unfair, I have to show him to you."

"I'm sorry, Wanjala," Lockery said. "I'm sorry you were embarrassed."

Wanjala rubbed his shoulder harder. "It is very unfair."

The woman in yellow touched his shoulder. He jerked away. She spoke softly to him, and though her face looked worried, her voice was edged in laughter. She beckoned with her hand for him to go into one of the huts, but he turned his face away.

"Was she inviting us to stay?" Lockery asked.

"'No."

"All right, we'll leave. But if you're lying about what she said, you'll be insulting her and her family," Lockery said. "And you'll be in trouble with me, too."

Wanjala cleared his throat. "She said we can stay if we want. Elija told her that. But he only wants to show us his daughter, the one who is with child."

"All right."

"I thought you would not be wanting to stay, Sir."

Lockery looked at Elija. Elija's eyes still burned, not with alcohol or hatred, but with the fierceness of an old man determined to hold and protect all he had until the day he dropped dead. Wrinkles deepened around his eyes, spreading all the way to his jaw. The man's face might have been carved in dark volcanic rock.

"Hell, yes—I want to stay," Lockery said.

The students sighed. Lockery decided not to hear them. Mwanga spoke up. "Sir, I can't feel happy to stay in this place. These people are uncivilized."

Lockery turned round. "Mwanga, you've been a pain in the ass all afternoon. At this point, I don't care if you're feeling happy or not."

"But, Sir—"

"Listen, Mwanga. One day you're going to be working in government. You'll be making decisions affecting the lives of people like these. You can't know what they need if you've spent your last ten years cloistered in boarding schools, soaking up 'civilization'. What the hell do you think you're being educated for—so you can quote Shakespeare in your love letters and ride around in a Mercedes impressing your friends?"

Mwanga glanced at the ground, then turned his face away and glared at the tree-tops. He did quote Shakespeare in his love letters. When he daydreamed, which was often, it was of riding around in a Mercedes impressing his friends. But what was wrong with that? Every student had similar plans. There was no point in spending all these dreary years in school if you didn't get a Mercedes at the end. Or at least a Ford Zephyr. When he graduated from university, he certainly wasn't going to ride around on a bicycle like a peasant or a crazy foreign teacher. He wanted to say something clever about bicycles and Mercedes, but he couldn't think of anything.

The woman in the sun-colored dress spoke to Wanjala. "Elija says we can come inside and take some beer," Wanjala said.

"May we drink beer?" Otieno asked. "We are off school grounds."

Lockery pretended to think for a moment. "We'd be insulting them if we refused. Right, Wanjala?"

"It is so, Sir," Wanjala said gravely, hiding a smile behind his hand.

"Let's have some beer, then."

The reception hut was cool and dark inside. It smelled of earth and cattle dung and of the dry thatch of the roof. Women set wooden chairs along the walls for the guests. A Victorian wicker armchair was brought in for Elija, but he did not appear for some time. The women moved silently, their bare feet padding across the mud floor. They were young women, and it was impossible to tell if they were Elija's wives or daughters or even grand-daughters.

One of them opened the wooden windows, letting in dusty beams of sunlight. A chicken fluttered noisily up onto a sill and perched there, clucking softly. It was a good sign, Lockery decided, that the chicken felt at ease enough to join the guests. The unruffled clucking sound calmed him. He began to sketch the interior of the hut, and instructed the boys to do likewise.

The only furniture besides the chairs was a heavy Pfaff sewing-machine console. It stood on curved ornate legs of black iron, guarding the door importantly. A lantern hung from one of the rafters. There were plates and cups and enamel pots on top of the walls, in the space below the roof. The walls were of red-brown mud, with vertical poles visible at intervals. On the walls were framed photographs. A family cluster. A shy bride in white who stood slightly off balance holding a heavy Bible. Two schoolboys in uniform, one solemn and stiff, one smiling painfully at the camera.

Lockery instructed each boy to write down nine questions to ask Elija. The questions were to be in three categories : life in the days of Flija's father and grandfather, life in Elija's younger days, and Elija's life during the last five years. "Use your imagination," Lockery said. "Ask good questions."

The students had rarely been asked to use their imaginations for a school assignment. They were puzzled and disturbed. Lockery showed them the questions he was writing in his notebook. Gradually they began working silently, looking about and tapping their pencils against their lips in concentration. Writing their own questions was harder than writing answers to someone else's questions, but it was more interesting.

Elija appeared in the doorway. He sat down slowly in his wicker chair. He looked round at the students and frowned. Wanjala explained that they were writing questions to ask him about his life. So well-respected was Elija that the school had sent the teacher and his students to collect his biography. Elija had never held a press conference before; he was torn between being suspicious and being flattered.

"*Sigara!*" he said, pointing at the pocket of the teacher's shirt. Lockery took out his Crown Birds and shook a cigarette part way out of the packet. Then, thinking again, he took out several cigarettes and held them out to Elija with both hands cupped, African fashion.

Elija stared at him. Then he roared with laughter.

The boys laughed, too. Wanjala explained: though it was indeed proper to offer food and most other gifts with both hands, it was not necessary to do so with cigarettes. Elija had seen a cigarette packet before. He knew that to take a cigarette you merely extracted it from the opening in the top.

Lockery felt his face reddening. He was so ignorant—what the hell was he doing here, really? His fingers shook as he lit Elija's cigarette. Elija did not stop chuckling until the end of the cigarette went up in flame. He blew it out, then he sat back and watched Lockery return to his seat as if he expected him to do a hand-stand for an encore.

"You have good intentions, Sir," Otieno said.

Lockery laughed. "I know. Sad, isn't it."

"No, Sir. It is good."

"Thank you, Otieno." Lockery composed his face. The chicken on the window-sill clucked cheerfully. "Oh, shut up," he said to it.

Wanjala smiled. It was Bukusu tradition, he explained, to bring a gift to the family of a new-born child. Elija's wife had just given birth to a son. She would be bringing it in shortly. Lockery took twenty shillings from his wallet. He told Wanjala to give it to the mother as a gift from everyone, with the compliments of the headmaster as well. Money was not the usual sort of gift, but judging from the look on Elija's face, it was a very acceptable gift.

The woman in the bright yellow dress appeared. She held a tiny brown baby in her arms. Elija beckoned her inside. She smiled shyly, glancing at her husband and then down at the ground at the feet of the strangers. Wanjala presented the twenty shilling note to Elija. Elija tucked it into the woman's hand. When Wanjala stood up to take a closer look at the baby, Lockery did, too. The baby stared hard at Lockery, the expression on its face poised between amusement and terror.

Lockery retrieved his notebook from the chair and tore out a page. Several barefoot children gathered outside the door to watch him fold the paper. They giggled when they saw the paper become a hat. Everyone laughed to see the baby with a hat on. Even Elija was smiling.

The baby squinted up at its mother, then burst into tears. She hugged it tight to her breast, laughing, the same look on her face she had used earlier to calm her husband. Elija raised his arm, and the look faded. The woman stepped backwards out the door, her eyes lowered, her smile private : a proper African wife once more.

On instructions from the teacher, Wanjala complimented Elija on his new son. Elija nodded solemnly.

The son was good. It was so. It was good to have children. Children were the real wealth of a man.

But if a girl had a child and she had no man to marry her, it was not good. Elija shook his head. No, such a girl could not bring many cattle for a bridewealth. Would a young man of a good family pay many cattle for the privilege of marrying a girl who was already spoiled? No. Only a young man of a poor family would ask for her. He would perhaps give only one thin cow. What was a father to give his own sons, then, that they might go and seek brides from good families? He would have but one thin cow to give his sons. Good families would not welcome his sons. They would say: Look, this young man has but one thin cow.

Elija shook his head. He tapped the floor with his walking-stick.

If Elija could not marry his sons into good families, people would say that Elija's family is not a good family. Did Elija want people to say that? No, he did not! Elija beat the floor with his walking-stick.

If Elija could not even force his daughter's abductor to pay the proper fine, people would say that Elija has become weak. Was Elija a weak man? No, he was not! Elija pounded the floor with his walking-stick.

Elija sat back in his chair, finished. Dark veins throbbed on his temples.

The chicken flapped its wings and dropped out of sight behind the window-sill. A feather fluttered slowly to the floor. The hut was very still,

"I think this is not a good time to ask him questions about his grandfather's life," Wanjala whispered.

Lockery swallowed hard. "You could be right."

Elija turned his head and shouted at the door. There was a flurry of footsteps behind the walls of the hut. Children who had been eavesdropping fled in all directions. "He wants to show you his pregnant daughter," Wanjala said.

But when the girl entered, Elija ignored the teacher. He clutched the girl by the wrist and pointed his walking-stick in Wanjala's face. He shouted at the girl.

Except for her full breasts, the girl looked no older than twelve. Her arm tensed across the little bulge in her belly, her fingers clutching at the faded material of her dress. No, she said, and turned her face away to hide her tears. No, he is not the one.

Wanjala sat back in his chair, still trembling. "I told you!" he whispered. "He should have asked her before he tried to strangle me."

"He wouldn't have gotten any information out of you, that way," Lockery said.

Elija glared at the teacher. He wanted the real father's name. He wanted the teacher to write the name on a piece of paper and give him the paper. Lockery lit a cigarette and puffed it slowly, stalling for time to think. "Tell him," he said, locking eyes with Elija, "that I cannot give the boy's name."

Elija did not wait for a translation from Wanjala. He pointed at the teacher's notebook, making writing motions with his finger.

Lockery wrote in his best legal English that he pledged to help Elija receive compensation for the loss of bride-wealth caused by his daughter's pregnancy.

When Elija demanded that Wanjala read him the letter in Bukusu, however, Wanjala added the boy's name, for good measure his two Christian names and his three Bukusu names. He promised, as he pretended to read the paper, that Mr. Lockery, himself, would deliver the boy to Elija within the week. Wanjala had no faith in the teacher's good intentions. Nor did he trust Elija not to send his sons after him one night, if the real father were not produced. The beating he would receive from this boy was nothing compared to the rage of Elija and his sons.

Elija mouthed the name of his daughter's seducer several times, committing it to memory. He had no faith in the teacher's promise, either. The paper was just to show the headmaster, when he visited the school later in the week. With the paper and the boy's name, he was satisfied. He saw the wisdom of his young wife—she had been right to calm his rage earlier. Of course, his rage had been wise, too. He had twenty shillings, a paper, and a name that had been authenticated by a European teacher. It was good. He had done well. Elija smiled.

He shouted out the door again. It was time to celebrate with some beer. Beer! he shouted. The visitors have seen Elija's new son, and now the visiting ritual can be resumed. Beer! Elija has been victorious, he shouted at the women as they scrambled to gather the calabashes of beer. Elija, who has never been to school—Elija, who cannot use a pencil or read from a book—Elija has defeated the teacher, the man who has studied in the universities of Europe! Let no man say that Elija is weak! Bring beer! Let no teacher, no schoolboys, say that Elija does not know hospitality! Bring beer! Let this herd of educated billy-goats hear the story of Elija Lukivya Waga, son of Waga Walumbe Chemai! Bring beer!

"Beer is coming," Wanjala translated. He took no consolation from the boys' smiles. He glanced uneasily at the teacher, but Lockery was grinning at Elija, and took no notice of him. "Elija is saying that he has defeated you," Wanjala said.

"Let him think so."

Wanjala stared at the teacher's face, The teacher did not look as if he had been defeated. Wanjala looked at the ground, shame-faced. "I told him the boy's name," he confessed.

"I know you did. I heard you."

"I was fearing him very much."

"I know. I was, too."

The women brought in beer in glass mugs. They

served Elija first, then the guests. The beer was thick and a little bitter.

"Do you like African beer, Sir?" Pius Otieno asked.

"Of course," Lockery said. "Did you ever meet a man who didn't like beer?"

"You see?" Wanjala said, turning to Mwanga and Ssanango, "Royalists are not the only ones who can make good beer."

Elija sat back in his chair and stretched his arms along the armrests. Tell your friends to get their pencils out, he said to Wanjala. Elija is ready for the first question.

KIKUYU WOMAN

I wave to her as I walk up the long path from the road, but she continues to stare motionlessly from behind the iron gate. The air smells of impending rain. Around her, the fields and trees glow with an eerie green light; it casts her face in deep darkness, but her body—her pale slacks, cardigan, and turban—radiates its own phosphorescence. Even as I draw close to her, her face remains shadowed, featureless. Then suddenly she is real. A bright smile cuts across her face, and the phantasm is gone. A woman stands there behind the gate, and we are greeting each other.

That smile, and the tribal scars on her cheeks: I remember Ruth not only from the restaurant last month, but also—I am sure this time—from about five years ago. Does she remember? I stare at her, but I can't tell. When her lips part to smile, her eyes wince and the tiny slits on her cheeks dart close together for protection.

I should be more fluent in Kiswahili than I am,

but I've been away from Africa, and am speaking awkwardly. Ruth changes to English. "Your family, Nairobi, they are all right?"

"My family isn't in Nairobi. They've gone back to America, but I'm staying here," I say, glancing down. "I have no family. *Kabisa*—finished."

She responds with a word I'm fond of, that means "I empathize": *"Pol-e."*

I nod. Then I give her my regards from Jerry and Wambui, our mutual friends from the restaurant. She thanks me politely, awkwardly.

"Well, you are here. So much time since we ask you. I think you not coming. I am glad now."

"I am, too." I smile, finally.

"It is little to welcome you to, this place—" She waves her hand in the direction of the yard. It is cluttered with rusty machinery, discarded parts of the tractors and combines that Lawrence, her husband, repairs for a living. A goat is lying in the sparse brown grass, chewing the remains of a doormat with a steady crunching sound. The air smells of diesel fuel and flowers.

Three houses stand in the yard: past, present, and future, I think. One is a thatched-roofed mud-walled hut, the original dwelling, now the kitchen. Against it sags an old wooden farmhouse with a rusted corrugated roof. The third is a new cement-block house with glass in the windows, and a hole in the tile roof where the chimney should be. I know that that house has never been lived in. Jerry and Wambui told me why. Lawrence had been hauling bricks for the chimney with his tractor; the tractor skidded sideways up an incline and toppled over, crushing Lawrence's leg. He dragged himself to the road, but by the time a driver saw him lying there, most of his leg was hanging out of the cuff of his overalls.

In the restaurant where I met him, Lawrence was sullenly quiet until Jerry mentioned that I was a writer. Then, interrupting the conversation, he spoke up to invite me to stay at his place over my school holidays. Everyone at the table stared at him, but he didn't seem to care. I learned nothing more about him from my friends, except that he is dying.

Every day now since I arrived, he lunges into the sitting room at tea time, sits by the fireplace, props his wooden leg up on a tractor engine block on the floor, and starts smoking and coughing and talking. I sit on the broken-down couch across from him and listen. Ruth serves us tea silently, gingerly, as if fearing that she might draw a glance from him and cause an explosion.

"I didn't give a damn if he was the Gov'nor, he was a bloody bastard," Lawrence says. "But I went over to him nice and polite, y'know, and I says, 'Evening, Gov'nor. I hope you're enjoying your stay up here.' And the bugger just turned his back on me!" Lawrence coughs hard, his leathery face wrinkling like an old yellowed map being unfolded. I expect to see dust fly out his mouth. But it's only phlegm. Splat—he spits against the back wall of the fireplace. "Y'see, they'd all told the Gov'nor I was a bloody African. For being married to a Kikuyu woman. . . ."

Kikuyu woman: I think of shaven-headed crones with dangling earlobes, trudging along roadsides in shapeless long dresses, bearing enormous bundles of firewood on their backs. And then I remember Ruth in the restaurant in Nairobi, in her tailored suit and white turban, ordering a daiquiri in defiance of her husband, sipping it slowly and sliding her tongue along the sugared rim of the glass. I cannot put her together in my mind. Especially because there is that other image of her, too: the loud shadowy dance floor, and the girls sitting at tables at odd angles to each other, their faces glazed with reptilian patience until a man enters and they flash smiles. . . .

I look up. Ruth is there in the room with us, setting a sugar bowl on the table in front of her husband. She pours his tea, carefully pours in milk and one level teaspoon of sugar. Then she straightens her body to watch him take the first sip.

"Excuse me," she says, ever so quietly. "Enough sugar?"

He says nothing at all. He does not nod or shake his head. He sets his cup down and glares at me.

Did he see me watching her breasts as she straightened up? I give him one of my blank artistic looks that makes people think me an absent-minded eccentric who notices nothing. It seems to work. He goes on with his story about the Governor.

"Excuse me," she says again, and waits for him to finish a long sentence. "Excuse me"—this time to me, with a smile. "Do you take sugar?"

"Yes. Yes, please."

She puts in two heaping teaspoons, and sets the cup and saucer on the table before me. Her eyes are lowered. "You like biscuits with your tea?"

Lawrence is frowning hard at her. I see a worried look on her face. Silence. Suddenly, I am certain there are no biscuits in the house, even though she has just offered me some.

"No, thanks," I say. "I'm not hungry."

She looks relieved. "Are you all right?"

"Yes, I'm . . . fine." I don't know what she means by "all right," but whatever she means, I am not particularly all right; I am hungry and restless, among other things. "You're not going to join us?" I ask her.

"My tea is in kitchen. I am cooking." She looks at her husband, moves toward a chair, stops, then walks silently toward the pantry door. She glances back at me, shaking her head just barely perceptibly. Does she remember me? All I know is that I must stop looking at her.

"Y'see, the Gov'nor wanted to find out if I was still in collusion with the Kikuyu," Lawrence continues. "Because I'd supported them during the Mau Mau—that's why the Colonial Office shipped me away to the Northern Frontier District in the first place. Thought they could get me to resign that way, and go back to the U.K." Lawrence laughs. "They weren't rid of me so easily!"

"So after the Emergency, you were still in touch with the Kikuyu groups?"

"After?" Lawrence's wrinkles bend into a ferocious frown. "The way those Kikuyu politicians sold out as soon as the war was over? Riding around the countryside in their Mercedes, ordering people about—worse than the bloody Colonials, they are. I wouldn't trust one of those politicians any further than I could throw that fireplace. And if it wasn't for this"—he raps his wooden leg, a startling hollow sound—"I bloody well could throw it further!"

I'm beginning to understand. As one of the rare Englishmen to support the revolution, Lawrence had expected a job with the new African government. But the government, now anxious to attract trade with Britain, found Lawrence an embarrassment. What happens to an old radical when his cause has been won and his former comrades are ordering wall-to-wall carpeting for their new offices? He is left in the bush to repair tractors.

"The trouble with these Kikuyu politicians, they've become culturally bastardized: half-castes, the lot of them."

As if on cue, his stepson Paul enters the room with an armload of firewood. He holds it carefully out away from his body and sets it down on the hearth. The old man watches the boy lean the split logs against the back wall of the fireplace, where he has been spitting.

"That wood's too long, at least half of it. Can't you even see that?" Lawrence sights along his stiff artificial leg at the wood. "You'll have to go out and cut it again."

Without a murmur, Paul sorts the long pieces out. Like his mother, he is immaculately clean. Blue shirt, gray short trousers, knee socks, and polished shoes: a model secondary school boy, except for his very pale brown skin. He is delicate-featured, with gentle calf-like eyes. An armload of wood does not go with his demeanor.

"I'll tell you in a minute if it's him cutting it or his mother," Lawrence says. We sit waiting. The shadows which have been creeping through the room have coated the walls entirely now, like soot. The walls have the cold stone look of a cave. The old man sits rigid, his head cocked to one side. I bite my lip, waiting for the catatonia-like spell to be broken. The room grows darker. Finally, I hear the chunk . . . chunk . . . sound of an ax striking wood, and let out all my breath.

"Well, I'll be damned. It's him this time." How can Lawrence tell, just from the sound? But he can.

"Usually he has her chopping the wood for him. Ruth's spoiled him rotten, that's his problem."

"He's terrified of you," I say.

Lawrence ignores me. "D'you know what those two did last year? Ruth brought in the wood one night herself. 'Where's the boy?' I asked her. 'Oh, he is outside,' she says, with that smile of hers—" He mimes Ruth's smile. On his wrinkled face, it is a hideous grimace. "Finally I got it out of her what happened. 'I let Paul stay outside. He want to live in rabbit hutch, because he annoy you too much,' she tells me. Gone to live in the bleeding rabbit hutch, he was! It's a bit of a circus around here sometimes." He shakes his head, coughs, and spits. "You want to hear more about the Mau Mau?"

I shift my position on the lumpy couch, trying to find a comfortable place. There isn't one. I've been sitting here for three hours. But listening to him is my meal ticket. Before I can reply, he starts another story.

Paul returns with the re-cut wood and lights the fire. Orange light flickers against the walls, and deepens the creases in the old man's cheeks. With Paul in the room, Lawrence's voice sinks to a conspiratorial tone which at times is indistinguishable from the hiss and crackle of the flames. I sense that I am in a cave with a tribal elder who is telling tales around a campfire. An elder without a tribe, for all tribes have become strangers to him. I am being lured into the conspiracies he unfolds, urged to join his lost tribe, one I fear that I may have joined already. The school where I teach is shut down and empty; I won't go back to my own country, nor will I go to Nairobi, where I would stumble into memories of my departed family. So I sit suspended here on this couch—for no other reason than that I was invited to be somewhere by another human being.

Ruth enters silently, a glow among the shadows. She moves close to the couch and waits. "Supper," she says finally, hearing a break in Lawrence's monologue.

We sit at the table. I hear the creak of feet on the pantry floor—her feet. I listen to the voices from behind the door—hers and Paul's. Is she telling him about me? I hope not. She is speaking in a local dialect which Lawrence evidently does not understand, for her voice is loud, urgent, as if she is pouring out secrets she has kept for so long that they have begun to fester. Suddenly Lawrence shoots a glance at the pantry door. The voice behind it sinks away quickly to a muffled whisper. What happened?

She comes in with a tray of food: potatoes and sausage, a European meal in my honor. It tastes like paste.

Ruth asks polite questions about my school to fill the long moments of silence. I cannot look at her, nor she at me, for the pressure lantern is between us on the table and to look up from our plates at each other would singe our eyes with the glare. Lawrence, at one end, can look at both of us. He does, regularly, between mouthfuls. Paul, at the other end, hardly eats, he is so busy watching us.

"What do American people do for enjoyment?" he asks. "Is it true that hippie girls have loose morals?" "Did you go to dances when you lived in England?" "Did you have a television? What was it like?" "Did you ever meet any Beatles?"

His questions are the important ones, and my answers to them are the ones Ruth listens to most attentively. I try to flavor my answers with glamour and excitement, and she gulps them down with the hunger of one who is just remembering how to taste what she swallows.

After supper, there is nothing to do but drink yet more tea and go to bed. My bed is a maize-husk mattress on a wooden frame. The room is cluttered with oily machine parts and smells of diesel fuel. As I lie down, my mattress crackles. On the other side of the wall, I hear Lawrence coughing his guts out, and I hear another mattress crackling. Soon I know it is Ruth on the other side of that thin wall, moving about in the bed inches from me to try to find a calm spot beside the coughing old man. I lie awake, listening to her crackling until dawn.

During the days, I am alone in the house with my typewriter and the spare parts of farm machinery lying about in every room. The land outside the open window is lush and green, shaded by tall peeling gum trees and flowering bushes, but I cannot escape the smell of diesel fuel. I give up working on my book, and just keep a journal. I write down the stories Lawrence has told me, and I write about Ruth—mostly minutely detailed descriptions of her. They are in the spirit of ancient cave paintings drawn by someone who thought that if he captured a creature's likeness in symbols, he would magically have good luck on the hunt later. I also write a prose poem about a caterpillar that is impatient to become a butterfly; once it becomes beautiful, however, it discovers that it must keep flying almost perpetually, unable to find a place on the earth to settle.

One day, I take a trip with Ruth and Lawrence to the farms and cooperatives. They visit one after another, he poking about beneath the machines with his tools, she keeping the accounts in a large ledger.

Since she speaks the local dialect, she must collect the farmers' payments. She parks the car along some rutted byroad and gets out; he watches her make her way across the furrows in her clean slacks and cardigan and turban. The men, sweating and dirty with their machetes resting at their sides, stare at her secretly. Some of them call her *memsahib*, the colonial word for "lady." She tries to banter with them, smiling and laughing; they smile back but remain silent. When a man does return her pleasantries, Lawrence leans on the car horn. An angry honk blasts over the quiet fields, startling the children from their play, causing women to pause in their hoeing for as far out along the fields as the eye can see. Ruth rushes back toward the car, clutching her ledger against her chest.

"What'd that blighter want, anyway?" Lawrence demands when she gets in.

Biting her lip, Ruth jams the car in gear and shoots back out the road in reverse, spraying mud from beneath the tires.

It is the same scene at every farm. One day of going around with them is enough. I prefer the empty farmhouse.

On Friday, as I am working, I see Paul coming round the side of one of the storage huts in the yard. When he sees me, he ducks back out of sight. Why is he hiding from me? I call out to him through the window, and he shyly reappears.

"My stepfather says I am not to bother you while you write," he explains.

"You don't bother me," I tell him. "I'm restless, anyway, I was thinking of walking into the village. Want to come?"

He thinks for a moment, staring hard at the ground. "Yes. I am also restless."

There is little to see in the village: two rows of Indian shops, each selling identical dusty merchandise—farm implements, packets of sugar and tea, plastic combs. Also several "hotels"—dim barrooms with tables and chairs at odd angles on the uneven cement floors. Here is where the town's only social life goes on. I offer to buy Paul a beer and his eyes light up, but he refuses.

"Europeans do not go into these places," he says.

"This European has been many places Europeans don't go." I laugh. "Unless you think the people inside wouldn't like to see me come in."

"No, no. They would like you. But it would be known all over the village that I brought a European into a hotel. My stepfather, he hates such places.",

"He'd be angry with you."

"Yes. . . ." Paul narrows his eyes, thinking. "But if we go to the post office, we can have a good reason for coming into the village."

"I'd rather not." I look at his face. "Oh hell, come on."

I buy Paul a beer, which he drinks happily, and then we go to the post office. As I feared, there is a letter for me. My headmaster wants me to return to school early—today, in fact—to help prepare the next term's schedule of classes. I'm furious about this. The letter tells me that he wants me to be acting assistant head next term, which will mean additional, tedious work at no salary increase, an end to the "non-essential" creative writing class I started, and less time for my own writing. If I refuse, he will get me transferred to some remote region as a way of getting me to resign. I came back to this country to write, but there's no way for me to survive unless I can do things that Africans aren't being trained to do yet, like doing school administration or repairing tractors.

When I tell Paul about my letter, he walks along beside me in silence, his face suddenly gone sad. "Will you go back to America?" he asks, finally.

"It seems inevitable, but—" I see a dead muffler on the roadside and kick it as hard as I can; it caroms off a tree stump and clatters back onto the roadside in an explosion of flaked rust. "No! There's nothing for me there." Ruth, too, is sad when she hears my news, but her face barely shows it. Lawrence, standing beside her, says, "Well, I hope you got a lot of writing done here." He drops his voice. "Did you, y'know, get it all down?"

I nod, understanding why he invited me here. "I've got it all down, yes."

He grins, all the creases in his face rushing to the corners of his mouth. I smile back, feeling like a bastard. He says good-bye—though I'm not to leave until later—because he has to go out to his workbench to do some blacksmithing before the afternoon rains start.

Today, for the first time, I eat lunch with just Ruth and Paul. Ruth has cooked cabbage, beans, and potatoes and left some for Lawrence on the charcoal brazier in the kitchen hut. We eat more slowly without Lawrence present. There are fewer questions and answers; we find ourselves laughing a lot, getting almost giddy at times. Ruth's yanked-mouth smile is gone; when she laughs, her pink tongue flashes and tears come to her eyes. "I am very glad you come for visit," she says suddenly.

Paul agrees. "No one has come since—" And he glances in the direction of the new house, then quickly away, as if the place contained explosives.

Ruth fetches a bottle of passion-fruit squash she has been saving "for a treat." Paul takes our bowls out to the kitchen, and discreetly closes the pantry door behind him, shutting off our view of Lawrence at his workbench. We can still hear him, hammering away steadily and furiously, but the sound seems farther away.

Ruth stretches back in her chair, her hands clasped behind her turban. Her breasts stand up inside her cardigan, sharp and full, as if they would like to fly. I am looking at her and she is smiling back at me. Then we hear a particularly loud outburst of hammering, followed by deep coughing. She drops her arms.

"Here, finish squash," she says, pouring the last of it into my glass. "I have to throw away bottle before he comes in. That man, he can't like to spend money. If he find bottle, he say, 'Why you buy this rubbish, stupid woman? We not having money for rubbish like this.' Is nonsense—he have money. Many many many shillings!"

She stretches her hands out to show the extent of his money, then drops them to the table. Her fingers twine and untwine around her glass, as if she cannot get a good grip on it . "He never like to go out, spend money. You know that time we meet you in restaurant, with Jerry and Wambui? He don't want to come. But I tell him, 'No, Jerry and Wambui, they old friends. They can be insulted, we don't take lunch with them. You know they helping us with Paul, to find school for him.' All right, he agree—but only for lunch. Wambui say to me in my language, 'This afternoon, we go shopping. We look at clothes.' I say, 'Wambui, you don't know how lucky you are, here Nairobi. You got shops, cinema, hotels, friends. My husband, he European like yours, but he can't like Europeans. He married to African, but he can't like Africans. So I can't stop with you this time, because he want to get back up-country hurry-hurry.'"

She shakes her head slowly. Her eyes are boiling over.

"Up-country here, I wait for him feeling good, then I say, 'You know, I working hard this week, I want to go out now.' He look at his watch and he say, 'One hour.' When he give me one hour, I double it!" A flicker of a smile appears on her lips, and vanishes. "So I go Kiganjo, Nyeri, Karatina, meet my friends. We are talking, that's all, but time goes. You have to greet people properly, you can't just say hello, then good-bye, yes? Is good to have friends. Myself, I like to have friends. But when I come home two hours, he looking at his watch. He say, 'Why you taking so long time, woman?' He say thing to me—*aaaagh!*"

The sound she makes cuts through the air like a machete. I lean forward over the table. Her face is clenched hard, eyes almost as narrow as the slits in her cheeks.

"My friend, if I was free, I could show you many places here. We could go to hotels—you like them? Good. Sometimes I go to hotels, meet friends. We talk, drink, we dancing and enjoying. Is good to have friends. Him, he don't have any. But myself—" She stops, and stares at me. "You don't tell him I go these hotels, all right?"

"All right," I say, and her face relaxes for a moment.

"You know, he is old man. Doctor say, he don't live one month—that five months ago. I think he afraid he going to die somewhere there is no one to bury him. So he want to die here, his place. Perhaps then, then we move into new house."

Suddenly she slaps her hands over her face. Her fingers slide down her cheeks slowly. "I feel sorry."

I touch her hand. It is wet.

"He work hard for us," she says finally, glancing in the direction of the hammering. "But the waiting. Waiting. I never know what day. . . ." She clutches at her chest, her fingers curled. "You ever wait like that?"

"I waited for my marriage to die. For years." I stare out the window. "And now, I feel as if I'm waiting for something again. I don't know what I'm going to do."

"Is not good." She picks up her glass again, her fingers twining and untwining. "Myself, I'm not going to die now. I'm not. I can't feel all right, just staying here all the time. But he always thinking, if I go out, I get special friend. All the time he worrying I going to go with somebody. So he watch me very close. But I can't agree for that. I can't!"

She stares at me hard. I say quietly, *"Pol-e.* I know."

Her lips part. She lets out all her breath, luxuriantly. Then she wipes her eyes. "Yourself, school where you stay—you sometimes get lonely?"

"Yes."

"You know, sometimes is good to have girl friend to help you. Special friend."

"I know."

"You have girl friend now? Which kind, European or African?"

Ruth is looking at me sideways, and simultaneously she seems to be glancing directly behind me at the door to my room. Where there is a bed. With a maize-husk mattress on it that crackles. That would crackle like a brush fire with the two of us on it. I have seen that look on her face before. I think, No, I don't want a quick one on that bed, with your husband who can see through doors hovering outside with his hammer clanging away at the air around us. I've had too damn many quick ones, that's why I'm so goddamn lonely. At the same time, I'm thinking that I have only to stand up and put my hand there on her shoulder and in an instant we would be crackling on that mattress....

"Perhaps you don't want to tell me," she says, still watching me.

"No, no. It's not that—" The truth is, I have a different "girl friend" every time, and she is usually African. But I don't want Ruth to remember me from five years ago. I don't want her to think I am the kind of European who hangs around bars looking for girls late at night, even though that is the kind of European I am. "I have no one right now," I tell her finally.

I look up at her. It's unnaturally quiet. Suddenly we hear the sound of the wind in the gum trees. The green tint is returning to the air in the electric silence before the rains.

"Lawrence, he stop hammering. That mean he want me to bring him lunch," she says.

"Come back, though, will you?"

She doesn't answer. At the door, she pauses and turns around. "You enjoy lunch?" she asks in a voice pitched to be overheard. "Are you all right?"

"I enjoyed lunch." I lower my voice. "But I'm not quite all right."

"I know," she whispers, and hurries into the kitchen.

I drink the last of my passion-fruit squash slowly,

to occupy the time. Then I pack my typewriter and suitcase, and bring them back to the table and sit down, and stare out the window at the darkening green hillsides.

Finally she comes back. "He say you must go now or you miss bus."

"I don't think I want to take the bus."

"How you can go? There is just one bus today."

"I'll hitchhike."

She smiles. "Like a hippie?"

"I'll turn myself into one." I tug down my hair over my ears. "Magic."

"I think you can turn yourself into many things."

I reach into my typewriter case for proof of my magic powers. "I wrote this for you," I tell her, and lay a piece of paper on the table before her.

She looks puzzled. "Lawrence say you are writing about him, his stories."

"Yes, but about you, too. Read it."

She looks down and shakes her head.

"You don't want to?"

She raises her eyes slowly. "I don't know reading."

"But that ledger?"

"Oh, yes, I learn numbers. And some words—machine words. I learn them for my husband, to help him." She sighs. "But I am village girl. My mind is clever for numbers, and I can wear these clothes, but I don't go to school. Never."

I stare at her. I am a writer and she cannot read. What the hell am I doing in this country? But what, more importantly, am I doing right now?

Finally she speaks. "You can read that paper for me. Paul, he reads letters for me."

I pick up the paper, then put it down again. "Another time, perhaps. . . ."

I stand up and rest my hand on her shoulder. She smiles suddenly. My fingers tighten gently, feeling the warmth of her. We walk to the door and lean against it, so that no one can walk through and surprise us. I relax my hold on her for a moment to look at her, and then I kiss her: her mouth, her chin, her cheeks. The slits on her cheeks feel hot against my lips. I hold her tight, trembling even more than she is. She feels warm and beautiful to me; she does not feel familiar, and I am glad.

"I can kiss like a European, with my tongue," she whispers. "You like that?"

"Yes, do you?"

"Anything." And she kisses me like a European. After a long time, she pulls her face back. She is listening. The hammering has not resumed. Suddenly we hear coughing from behind the door.

"He want me to do ledger with him," she says. "Take suitcase now."

I pick up my suitcase and typewriter. But he doesn't come in.

"We have a minute," she says. "We say good-bye. But perhaps you come back."

"I don't know."

"Why you don't?"

"I have to tell you. I've been with you before. We met in Nairobi, at the Flamingo Club. Then at your flat in Bahati. You remember?"

"No."

"It was five years ago."

She nods. "That was after the war. There were many Europeans Nairobi then. I don't remember you. Sorry."

"No—I'm glad."

"Why? You ashamed?"

"Yes. But not now. It's different now."

"Good."

We hug each other close. I can smell her hair beneath her turban and it smells sweet. She looks up at me suddenly. "Shame is for weak people. After the war, people like me, they have to do things they don't do before, so they can eat. People with shame, they just starve. Myself, I don't want to starve."

"I don't either," I say, and my fingers touch her hair beneath the turban.

Since I have missed the bus, I don't hurry. Paul wants to show me the new house Lawrence built and the garden, and so we go outside. I'm curious to see the house.

We enter through the front door. There in the foyer sits a big bathtub, unconnected to anything. Its pipes poke out over the edge every which way like arteries and veins in a model of a heart. As I stare at it, a goat bounds in behind me, past me, and disappears around a corner. Paul and I follow the goat into each room. There is nothing in the house at all. It is dark. The empty rooms smell of cement and thick dust that makes us cough.

"This is my room—see how big it is," Paul says. "And this is the kitchen—it's very modern, you see the taps?"

Except for the sink, the kitchen looks like the other rooms—four walls, a cement floor, a ceiling. In one wall there is a crack from ceiling to floor, like a stroke of lightning. Flakes of plaster crunch underfoot.

Paul kneels beside the sink and opens a cabinet. "I have been keeping my rabbits in here, now that the rainy season is starting." A timid gray rabbit face appears and nuzzles the palm of his hand. "Please—you won't tell my stepfather?"

Another secret. I promise not to tell Lawrence about the rabbits living in his mausoleum. "But let's go, shall we?" I say.

What Paul calls the garden is several fields of once domesticated flowers and tall peeling gum trees beside a river. The garden is very quiet; the hammering from the workbench up the hill hardly reaches us. The sun comes out briefly, brightening the colors. We walk among huge wild stalks, higher than my head, some of them with incredibly brilliant yellow flowers at the tops, like cornucopias. At our feet are tiny flowers with blue and white petals, no larger than the heads of jeweled pins. Beyond a grove of trees, a river winds calmly through chaotic snarled underbrush, sparkling and murmuring. If only I had known about this place before. Ruth and I might have come here. . . .

Paul keeps asking me questions, distracting me. He wants to know about foreign teen-agers and astronauts and marijuana and racing cars and gangsters. I give in, and tell him more tales of the exotic West. His eyes grow bright, and as we walk along I find myself smiling back at him.

Before we leave, I pick a pale red-orange flower. Then we climb up through a pasture toward the three houses. When we reach a barbed-wire fence, Paul holds the wires apart for me, then I hold them for him. He sees the flower in my hand.

"That is a nice one," he says.

Now that he has noticed it, I don't know what to do with it. "I just picked it." I say.

"I can show you some more, when you come back next."

I look back toward the garden.

"Were you wanting to give that flower to my mother?" he asks.

"Yes." I was going to. But we have already said our good-byes. I can't think—the clanging from the workbench is ringing in my ears. I can see Ruth sitting near it on the ground with the ledger in her lap. The flower... a hopeless gesture. Like writing words on a piece of paper. But she asked me to read it to her, didn't she?

"Perhaps she'd like the flower," I say to Paul, who has been watching me.

"Oh, yes." He reaches out for it. I give it to him and he tucks it carefully under his clean shirt. "I can give it to her for you. Like a message. Until next time."

I smile. "All right."

We walk on up the hill past the new house. Hearing a muffled *baa*-ing from inside, Paul opens the front door. Then we laugh as the goat charges out and, snatching up great mouthfuls of grass with its teeth, bounds around us in wide delirious circles.

GIVE ME TIME

I take my eyes off daughter for only a second. When I turn back, I see her stumbling toward the cliff. I lunge forward, but she has fallen over the edge. Standing in horror, I can hear no scream or thud in the darkness below. The air throbs with silence as if I'd never known her at all.

    I hadn't had this dream for years, since Jill was a toddler, but in clear daylight one Saturday in New York, the memory of it rushed back with a force that knocked the breath out of me. One moment my daughter and I were waiting on 48th Street for a matinee to start... and the next moment, she was gone. Since I only got to see her holidays and two weekends a month, I usually focused all my attention on her, but today I'd been distracted by a letter I'd received from Africa. Now I shoved through the crowds searching for a small just-thirteen-year-old girl with curly yellow hair, bright eyes, braces on her teeth that flashed when she smiled. What had she been wearing? New blue jeans, a purple blouse. Anything else? A striped fuzzy shoulder bag in the shape of a zebra; she'd had it since childhood, when she'd stuffed pajamas in it for over-nights. Seeing people gathered around a spot near a construction fence, I hurried toward it. And there she was, shuffling out of the crowd.

I wanted to laugh with relief, but I just hugged her. She was taller than I'd pictured her a few seconds ago. "Are you all right?"

"Sure," she said. But I could feel her trembling like a bird that's flown into a window pane.

"Where'd you go?" I asked.

"There." She pointed to the fence. Before a backdrop of old posters, a seated man was flipping three cards so fast his hands blurred above the cardboard box on his knee. "Step up! Follow the Jack, double your money! Five, ten—all right—twenty!" He turned over a card, pretending to groan; it was a Jack that a woman, his shill, had pointed to. He held up two twenties for her to grab.

"Did you give him any money?" Jill shook her head against my chest. "I won't be mad, if you did."

"I was just watching," she said. Her voice was scratchy.

"Did anybody touch—"

"No, nothing like that." She shook her head.

"Then what's the matter, honey?" I heard no reply. The chimes from the theater started. I glanced at my watch; the play was about to start. "Do you want to tell me about it? Or wait till the intermission?"

She wiped her eyes. "Intermission."

We went in. I stopped glancing at Jill to see if she was all right when I saw her laughing and getting involved in the play, a romantic comedy. But I wasn't concentrating on it, myself. I couldn't stop remembering Africa, and the letter in my jacket pocket that weighed like a flat stone against my chest.

*   *   *

The letter was about a woman I'd known named Lorena. I recalled the first time I saw her standing on the lawn outside a friend's house in Nairobi, Kenya, about a dozen years before. Her hair glowed dark red; she brushed long wavy strands from her face. As she turned slowly, everything she saw brought wide curious smiles to her face—the party guests murmuring in several languages on the terrace, the bell-shaped flowers in the garden, the marmalade cat under the bush. Beneath the hem of her cotton dress I saw bare white toes curling in the grass. If I were the cat, I'd pounce on them, I thought. She walked in my direction into a patch of sunlight. I stepped forward to meet her there.

The next day I borrowed my friend's Land Rover and drove Lorena up to the Ngong Hills to show her a view of the Great Escarpment. In a valley in Tanzania like this one, I'd spent five years as a Peace Corps teacher during the euphoric period following the success of the African independence movements; then I'd returned to the States for several years, and now had just come back. I'd let my hair grow shaggy again, and had on my old village teacher outfit, khakis and denim shirt. That afternoon, the sun left a gold tint on the grass nearby. The valley below resembled an ancient ocean floor; it radiated a pale green that darkened to purple where the mountains rose like mounds of coral in the distance.

"What do you think?" I said, proud of finding her this place.

"Amazing. The air seems to be trembling." She raised her hand before her face, fingers wide to catch the vibrations.

I heard them, like a vast hum. "All those thousands of people, moving around down there."

We sat down in the grass together to talk. After a while, three very tall Masai men strode by in tablecloth-checked togas. They carried spears and their bare black arms and legs glistened in the sunlight; with their dung-hardened hair, they looked as if they were wearing black ostrich eggs.

Lorena leaned against me. "Masai warriors?" she whispered

"Well, herdsmen these days." I told her that until recently the Masai had raided other tribes for cattle; they still lived on a diet of cow's blood and milk. At a distance, the three men stopped to watch us, murmuring as if they expected us to do something dramatic at any moment. Then they gave up and loped off down the hillside. The air behind them remained charged with their curiosity.

Lorena and I talked all afternoon sitting there in the grass. We took each other's hands as we brought up difficult subjects. One was that we were both married. We need to say that, and then quickly put it behind us. Lorena was twenty-five, she said; her big brown eyes tilted at the corners, making her look older. She was divorcing her husband; he drank a lot and had a girl on the side. She'd started doctoral work in anthropology and had come here to look into field work opportunities. I told her I was thirty-three and my marriage seemed to be almost over, too, though I had no complaints about my wife other than being sick of her understandable impatience with me for not settling down at anything. For several years, we'd tried hard to have a child; then we pretty much stopped trying. I'd come back to Africa, where I'd once felt purposeful and happy, to see if I wanted to live here for good.

When I took Lorena back to my friend's house, he was gone for the night; the cook served us in the dining room and tiptoed away. We listened to his footsteps fade on the driveway outside the window; then we turned to each other and smiled. The house was ours.

When we lay together on the couch later, she told me, as if to warn me, that her husband thought she was too big. I said no, she was just right for me—especially here in Africa, where nicely rounded women like her were cherished. I remembered then how my wife's breasts shrank—willfully, it seemed—to the vanishing point when she lay on her back; in bed that night, Lorena's quivered happily as she snuggled against me.

Later that week, when we went camping, I watched her slip naked into our sleeping bag, and told her that she was graceful. "That's new, then," she said, blushing. As she leaned over me, her hair fell light and soft against my face. We both said we felt sexier than we ever had before. It helped that our love-making took place under vast starry skies in game parks where breezes smelled of pacing lions and rang with elephants' trumpeting. I began to feel worthy of her roiling sobs of gratitude, the likes of which I'd never heard before in my life.

Back in Nairobi, she told me she might be falling in love with me, and I said I was feeling the same way. Then, strangely, we both received letters from our spouses at the post office that day. As we sat on its stone steps reading them, dissonance swarmed around me like a flock of tiny screeching birds. My wife's handwriting on the blue aerogramme was the same slanted script that, when I was just getting to know her, I read with growing fascination. And now I missed her—that young woman who had agreed to marry me many years ago. And yet I longed all the more for the fascinating young woman sitting beside me now.

Amada looked up from her own letter. "It's so disorienting!"

"I know," I said. "Have you ever done this before?"

She shook her head, trying to laugh, and wiped her eyes with the sleeve of her blouse. "Have you?"

"Innocent."

"I wonder if our lives are going to change," she said.

"Well, we've got time to decide." I had an open return ticket, and Lorena's flight to the States was five weeks away—if she decided to take it. Five weeks seemed like forever, a golden age, a gift.

I'd learned that foreigners weren't being hired as teachers in Tanzania any longer, but I filled out a job application at the Kenya Ministry of Education and Lorena spoke to professors at the university. Before any hiring decisions could be made, we were both told, transcripts had to be sent for and paperwork had to be processed. Meanwhile, she was eager to go with me to the village where I wanted to visit my former students. A friend drove us to the border near the coast, where we exchanged our Kenya money for Tanzanian shillings at a little brick bank next to the customs office. But African hospitality insured that we'd never pay for a meal or a room; we slept happily on corn-shuck mattresses and woke at dawn as an impatient rooster crowed at us from the open doorway. The scent of wood smoke drew us outdoors; we watched the mist turn silver on the fields in the first rays of the sun. Children shouted somewhere; a cow mooed; someone chopped wood. These were like the sounds I'd heard faintly from the Ngong Hills; now I was right among them again—where I'd dreamed of being ever since I'd left the country. I loved helping Lorena get to know the place as I had years before. I explained customs, I taught her phrases in Kiswahili. No one had ever been so interested in the things I knew. She even wrote them in her journal.

Eventually I grew restless without a job to do in the village where I'd once worked so hard. Lorena and I decided to travel for a while. The scruffy hotels we found seemed romantic. We enjoyed the slow rides on elderly buses, and happily slept a night on the roof of one that broke down miles from anywhere. We camped on a plain near Mt. Kilimanjaro, where we once saw a rainbow that seemed to fall just down the path from us.

Once, waking up, she asked me what time it was, but I had to tell her I didn't know; I'd left my watch, an old cheap one, at the house in Nairobi with my suitcases. Then the next day, in the city of Tanga, she asked me the same question. When I said again I didn't know, she sighed and shrugged, her eyes tilting for a moment with a disappointed expression. So when I saw a man selling watches from a plank table in a dockside market, I stopped to look. They were good ones, no doubt fallen from the back of a truck or from one of the graceful square-sailed *dhows* floating in the harbor. One in particular caught my eye; its bright silver dial throbbed in the sunlight. The man quoted me a price. Glancing at Lorena, I offered a quarter of it. He feigned a grimace, his forehead wrinkling; then he came down five shillings, then ten. In a few moments I was bargaining with him like the expert I'd been years before. Lorena watched me admiringly. I could feel sweat trickling down my forehead. The merchant finally came down to half his asking price. Then the watch was glittering in the palm of my hand.

* * *

When my daughter and I reached the sidewalk during the play's intermission, she blinked in the sunlight, staring up the street. The place where the crowd had gathered was now just empty sidewalk. The construction fence was a mess of new posters plastered over faded and shredded ones, a palimpsest collage of black and red letters, a mouth, stained bodies. The stricken look was back on Jill's face, her eyes narrowed, her lips turned down at the corners.

"Are you remembering what happened before the play?" I asked.

She nodded, turning slowly toward me. "I lost my bag."

"The zebra bag?"

She nodded. "I was watching the card game the guy was playing. The bag was hanging from my shoulder by its strap. Then the next moment it wasn't there."

"That's terrible, Jill," I said.

"I should have told you," she said. "It's just that, I mean, I didn't even feel it slip away. I looked everywhere, but it was *gone*. Forever!"

I put my arm around her shoulder. "I'm sorry. What there a lot in it?"

"Just a few bucks, a hairbrush, a magazine. It wasn't that." Jill stamped her foot. Her curls jiggled on the smooth skin of her forehead. "It was the bag. I loved it. I thought I'd always have it."

"The fuzzy zebra." I felt sad, too. I remembered giving it to her years before. "You'd had it since you were pretty young."

"I was probably too old for it—I know.."

"I didn't mean that." I wondered what I should do now. Offer to get her a new one?

She walked over to the fence and begin tearing away strips of paper, wadding them up and throwing them down. Now she looked embarrassed that I'd seen her—no child wants a parent to witness her loss of innocence—and she walked past me back into the theater. When I joined her at our seats, she kept her face turned away, buried in the program.

* * *

The watch I'd bought in Tanga kept exasperatingly accurate time. As soon as Lorena and I woke up, it told us how many hours we had left together in the day. Lying in bed at midnight, we could almost hear the click of the date changing in its little window. The watch was the first thing I took off when we stripped to make love.

We took trips to game parks, we camped on beaches, we visited more people I'd known several years before. They were glad to see me, but they were busy with their jobs, families, lives; I was just a visitor from abroad, now. In Dar es Salaam, Lorena and I splurged on a hotel where we could hear the Indian Ocean lapping at the rocks beneath our window. The city was, as its name said, a haven of peace, with lovely palm-lined streets, graceful mosques and lively markets. The problem was, it made us wish we could stay longer. But now we'd gone as far as we had time for; in only three days Lorena had to either take her flight from Nairobi or cash in her ticket.

We took a road back to Kenya through the Masai country to the west. The sun was almost white in the sky above the tree branches, its heat turning the dust to fiery powder. When the bus made stops, the breeze was sucked away into the still afternoon, leaving us drenched with sweat.

"I never went back to the Ministry of Education in Nairobi," I told Lorena. "I'll do it first thing."

"I never checked back at the university, either."

"We got distracted." I smiled.

She rested her head on my shoulder. "We sure did."

"The thing is, though, I'm beginning to wonder what I'm doing here."

"Me, too."

"I'm skimming over the surface of the country," I said . "I'm not connected to anything any more."

"Except me," she said. "But that's not enough, is it?" Then she sat up and squeezed my arm. "Don't answer yet—please."

In Arusha, the last town before the Kenya border, the only hotel room we could find had twin beds. Once I woke to see Lorena's silhouette watching me from her bed as if she were seated in a floating rowboat. In the chilly silver dawn light I found her asleep beside me, clutching the sheets to keep from falling off the narrow mattress. As I kissed her fingers, they grew warm against my lips. I took her in my arms to pull her close. We said that we loved each other, and every time we said it our eyes teared over and we rubbed our wet faces against one another and said it again and wondered if it were true.

Walking in the market the next morning, I wanted to buy Lorena a souvenir of Tanzania. We found a shop that sold beautiful printed cloths. The woman shopkeeper wrapped her in one with yellow clouds and maroon flying birds. She spun around slowly, holding it out and hugging it back around her body.

"You look lovely," I told her, "like a walking sky."

"Wow!" She flushed. "Okay. But I want to buy you one, too."

"Sure."

"Maybe," she said, "we could use it for a bedspread one day."

I chose one with leaping gazelles. We counted out almost the last of our Tanzania shillings—beautiful bank notes printed with gold-tinted mountains and valleys and animals. Like Lorena, I still had travelers checks in my luggage in Nairobi, but I was sorry to see these bills go.

Lorena went back to the hotel to wash her hair, and I continued walking aimlessly. I found myself standing in front of the town post office, a neat cinderblock cube with white-washed stones lining the path to the door. I remembered telling my wife I might come through Arusha if I went with friends to a nearby game park; it occurred to me that she might have sent a letter to me here. Once I thought of this, I couldn't move away from the building. It'd nag me the rest of the day if I didn't just check, I told myself. I walked in, showed my passport at the *poste restante* counter, and waited for the clerk to say, "Nothing for you." Instead, he handed me a blue aerogramme. He was smiling, until he saw my face. I took the letter to the window. My name was spelled out in a familiar slanting script. The only other hand-written words were: "Original sent to Nairobi." The rest was typed; I was holding a dim carbon copy. The words were like faint whispers. I stared at the one short paragraph, and noted that my wife hadn't signed it at the bottom.

Outside, the street looked blurred; shapes seemed blue-tinted as they moved strangely beside me. I smelled smoke from a cook fire, and somewhere a sewing machine whirred. I kept my eyes on the ground as I walked with a kind of floating motion. When I found myself back on the main street, the scene looked as if it had been painted on invisible boards—a backdrop, a mirage. Somehow, incredibly, I convinced myself that I didn't have to deal with the contents of the aerogramme until I saw the original, signed copy. The real letter. Hadn't all long-term plans been postponed until Lorena and I got back to Kenya? Yes, that was what we'd agreed to, and we couldn't change it now, here in Tanzania, before our trip was finished. I needed time to think. Then, once we were heading across the Kenya border, I'd have an important new insight. Or Lorena would think of something we hadn't discussed yet. Some law of inevitability would click in, and we would surely figure everything out.

In the hotel lobby, Lorena sat in an old armchair, her arms wrapped tight around her drawn-up knees. Her hair hung down, wet and heavy.

"Have I been gone long?" I asked.

"All my life," she said.

The bus to Kenya was dusty green with a rusted baggage rack on top. Sacks of potatoes, banana bunches, trunks and old suitcases were tried down with hemp rope. As the bus rolled out of town, I could hear the luggage straining overhead at every corner. Lorena gripped my hand as if that would keep the bus from tipping over.

Women suckled babies and dozed, their bare feet splayed out comfortably in the aisle. Across the aisle, two old men stroked chickens in their laps and talked quietly. A warm breeze blew through the windows; everyone seemed lulled into contentment. But as the bus slowed to a halt, a grumbling sound passed like a gray wave along the rows of seats. Even the chickens gave off a low, nervous clucking

Beside the road waited a group of very tall men with spears.

"Masai!" Lorena said. Her face was sunburnt, her lips cracked, but she still had a lovely smile.

The first man didn't just step onto the bus, he commandeered it, striding up the aisle and stopping to bang the blunt end of his spear against the floor as a signal for everyone to make room. Boxes and suitcases and burlap bags had to be shifted off seats. People leaned away from the new passengers; as the men crowded through, their togas pulled away from their thighs to reveal at face-level their black-iron thighs and dusty flapping penises. The air was filled with the smell of the cattle dung which the men had mixed with mud to fix their hard, oval hair-dos. With the dung came flies, which now buzzed around everyone. Lorena fanned them away from her face with her journal.

The tallest man crowded onto the end of my seat, took a pinch of snuff from a plastic film canister, and pushed it under his lower lip. He had high cheekbones, narrow eyes, and perfect white teeth. His spear stood upright between his knees. Lorena was wedged between me and the window as the bus lurched back onto the road. The conductor arrived selling tickets, and the new passenger pulled a roll of bills from his homemade cowhide wallet. I tried to make more room for Lorena on the seat. The man moved over a little, looking me in the eye. Then he tapped my arm hard with his forefinger.

"*Nipe saa,*" he said in brusquely-accented Kiswahili.

Nipe meant "give me" but *saa* I wasn't sure of. It could mean "time" or "wrist-watch." Give me time? *Saa ngapi* was the usual way of asking what time it was. My watch said Three thirty. I held it up for him to see.

He shook his head. "*Nipe saa!*"

"He wants my watch," I told Lorena, brushing away flies. Suddenly I was glad for this chance to get rid of the thing. But I didn't want to be bullied out of it. When the man took hold of my wrist to inspect the watch, I yanked my hand back. He showed me his bundle of money and counted out twelve ten-shilling notes.

"That's less than you paid for the watch." Lorena leaned closer to me. "What's he want a watch for? It's not like he has to go to meetings or make deadlines."

"True." I looked at my watch's glittering silvery dial, its gold numbers and burnished leather band, and I looked at the gold-tinted landscapes on the banknotes the man was holding in his huge hand. 'Maybe he just likes the way it looks," I said.

Lorena watched the man count out two more notes. "It must be hard to find something like that, all the way out here," she said.

I realized she wanted to be rid of the watch as

much as I did. The man counted out three more notes, the last one crisp and bordered with a filigreed design like some sort of graceful, exotic script. Suddenly I didn't want to bargain any more. He was offering what I'd paid for the watch. Now the bus was slowing down. People started lifting bags from the floor. I heard a murmur of voices around me—everyone seemed to be watching the transaction.

"*Saa yako,*" I said. "It's your watch."

The man plunked down his wad of bills into my hand and slowly took the watch from me. Dangling it in front of his face, he squinted at me for a second, a kind of smile, and I nodded back. Then he strode away down the aisle.

We'd arrived at the Kenya border.

As I waited in the customs queue beside Lorena, I saw the tall man from the bus striding away with his entourage. Evidently Masai didn't have to go through immigration; their semi-autonomous tribal territory was in both countries. A dozen or so people approached the man from the Kenya side; he must have lived nearby with his family. I watched him stop beneath an acacia tree whose branches spread above him like fan coral. He showed off a shiny strip around his wrist—my watch. Everyone crowded close: men with spears, old women in aprons and shaved heads, lots of nearly naked kids. Then they all walked on together. They followed no visible path, but I could tell that they knew exactly where they were going.

Lorena and I filled out forms, and I noticed how neat Lorena's handwriting was. As we walked away from the customs post, I had the floating sensation I'd had walking the streets of Arusha. I took the bills from my pocket and shuffled them slowly. A few were new and bright, and I could see the trees and flowers and clouds outlined sharply in their frames. Most of the bills were old—the same landscapes but in faded versions, the edges worn soft as flannel, the gold tint inevitably muted to sepia. I held them close to my face. The smell of cowhide on the paper was still fresh.

"Don't you want to change them for Kenya money?" Lorena pointed to a little brick building beside the customs shed.

"You can't change Tanzania shillings going this way over the border," I said. "No bank outside of Tanzania accepts them."

"You mean—?" She looked up at my face. "All those bills are worthless?"

"No." I shuffled them until the brightest one was on top, then pushed the roll deep into my pocket. "I've got what I wanted," I said.

From the bus window, we stared out over the open savanna, with its shimmering grass and branch-coral-like trees. I looked for the Masai family, but they were long gone. Once I pointed out some gazelles running across the plains in a valley below the road; Lorena barely nodded. Neither of us said anything about a rainbow in the distant mountains. The light was growing dim as the bus rolled into the industrial suburbs of Nairobi several hours later. I thought Lorena had been dozing, her face to the window, but now she turned to me, wide-eyed, awake.

"We're not going to stay here together, are we?"

"I want to, in so many way," I said. "If it were just you and me—"

"I knew it." She wiped her cheek with her sleeve. "It was like a shift in the wind."

"In Arusha I got a letter from my wife. I'm sorry, I shouldn't have waited so long to tell you."

Her shoulders twitched. She hit me in the chest, once, then her fist dropped to her lap. Her eyes were wet. "Do you miss her so much?"

Right now, I only missed Lorena, though she was still right beside me. "That's not it."

"Then what is?" Her voice cracked.

The bus tilted as it swung around a corner. "My wife wrote that if I wanted to stay here," I said, "she'd understand how restless I'd always been to go back to Africa. But...."

Lorena squeezed my arm.

"But she wanted me to know that she's pregnant."

Lorena took her hand away, and my arm felt as dead as the rest of me. She rubbed her eyes and sat up. Then without any rancor in her voice, she spoke about my decision for the last time, and I knew what I had lost. "Now maybe you and your wife can be happy together."

* * *

We were, for a while. We loved the baby, Jill. I found a job in New York that I actually liked. I learned that Lorena had stayed on in Kenya and eventually gotten her degree. "No regrets now," she wrote me about our affair, and we kept in touch by mail. The last I heard she was doing more field work, this time in Tanzania. I felt a sharp twinge as I pictured her there without me. My marriage to Jill's mother had ended by then, a remarkably amicable break-up. I wrote Lorena to tell her about the divorce, and asked if she'd like me to visit her. I said I'd even saved the beautiful Tanzania shillings from our last bus ride. But until I received the aerogramme today, about three years after my letter, I'd had no news of her.

The play ended with various couples uniting happily. If it had had a tragic ending, walking out of the theater might have been easier—the leaden feeling of something waiting for us outside wouldn't have come on so suddenly. I saw Jill's face fall when she stared down the empty sidewalk at the ragged fence. People rushed by us, going back to their real lives, and soon my daughter would be going back to hers, at her mother's house in the country.

"I wish I could have thought sooner what to do about your bag," I said. "Something's been on my mind."

"The play?" Jill asked.

I shook my head. "I got a letter today." Now I was on strange territory. I could see that Jill sensed it too by the way she pressed her knuckles to her lips. "It's about someone I knew a long time ago, someone I was fond of." I took out the folded blue aerogramme. Was I really going to show it to my daughter? Maybe she was grown up enough now. I handed it to her. "My friend's husband wrote it," I said.

He was a Tanzanian sociology professor who had evidently married Lorena several years earlier in Dar es Salaam. His script was as neat as hers had been. I was one of the people she had wanted him to write to. He was very regretful to inform me of her passing. But she had had good care and had not suffered at the end.

Jill stared at the letter long after she'd read it. On the smooth skin of her forehead were faint lines I'd never seen before. Finally she handed the paper back to me. "That's really too bad," she said softly. "I'm sorry."

"Thank you." I nodded, missing Lorena terribly. Then as if for the very first time—though it wasn't for the first time at all—I thought: if I'd stayed in Africa with her, Jill, I'd never have known you. And how could I ever have lived, not knowing you?

"So, anyway, " I cleared my throat. "The bag you lost—I know where they sell them, or used to, anyway. Do you want to go look for one?"

She glanced down. A faint smile lifted one corner of her lips. "No, I'll be okay."

"Are you sure?"

"Yes," she said.

And as we walked up the sidewalk with my arm around her shoulder, I wondered what I could possibly have had done to deserve such good women in my life.

MIRIAMU AND THE KING

On Independence night, the African Star Uhuru Bar was packed with celebrators.

"Every man in the village was in my bed tonight," Adija said. Adija and Salome were barmaids at the African Star. "Every man but the one I want."

"The whites are staying in their houses this night," Salome said.

"He'll come. You'll see." Adija lay on her side next to Salome. "He's not fearing me. I'm only half-African, anyway."

Adija's back was pale, pale brown in the glow of the lantern. Her bones stood out beneath her skin. Tiny ridges rippled up her spine. Salome's eyes hurt to look at them. She pulled the blanket up over Adija. "Are you very sore?" she asked.

Adija was rubbing oil into her crotch. She pretended not to hear. "You see that picture of the king?" she asked, pointing at the wall.

Salome looked. Adija's crazy collection. If you stick people to the wall with pins, Adija had explained, they can't move about or shout at you or behave badly. They just have to keep smiling. You can think they're trying to please you with their smiles. Salome searched for the picture of the king. Elvis Presley leered at her. Satchmo flashed his teeth. A fridge gaped, a television stared. Queen Elizabeth smiled at a procession of schoolchildren waving their Union Jacks. The country's cabinet ministers stood beside their new houses and motorcars. They were smiling.

There was the newspaper photograph of Adija's white man. He was standing on an airport runway with the other missionary teachers from America. Beside the photograph was a color picture of the king. He was sitting on his throne beneath a crown that looked too heavy for his delicate, brown face. "I found it," Salome said.

"Beneath it is the picture of Rita Tushingham." She was a famous film actress. "The one in the school uniform."

"It's not a school uniform. It's a servant's uniform."

"It's a school uniform," Adija said. "You want to hear the story, or don't you?"

"One of your stories," Salome laughed. "Yes, go ahead. It'll distract me."

"Miriamu was a poor schoolgirl," Adija began. She raised her hands as she spoke, in the manner of the Arab fishermen who lived in her home village on the coast, and told the following story.

The other schoolgirls mocked her, because she was poor. The men in her town called her a slut, because her father was an Arab trader. Her mother beat her, because she failed her examinations at school. But Miriamu was always happy.

One day all, the schoolgirls went to the palace of the king to shout their praises and wave their flags at him. The king had a beautiful big palace. It had four rondavels at the corners, with roofs of woven palm leaves, and high white walls between the rondavels. It was finer than the finest mosque in the city. The king stood on the wall and looked down at the schoolgirls. He was very bored with these parades of schoolchildren. He was not feeling happy that day, because he had not been out of the palace in it long time. But when he saw Miriamu he smiled. He said: "Here is the most beautiful girl in my kingdom. She is the one I am going to marry."

He sent his ministers to discover who the beautiful girl was.

"Her name is Miriamu," said the Minister for Commerce.

"But she is too ignorant. She is thin and her skin is a strange, pale color," said the Minister for Home Affairs.

"She is not good enough to marry a king. You must marry a girl of a royal caste," said the Minister for Information, Tourism, and Wildlife.

"I am the king," said the king.

"If you marry her," said all the ministers together, "we will plot a coup to overthrow you."

"Really, I think she is good enough," said the king.

The ministers all whispered together. "If you wish to marry her, we will have to test her." said the Minister for Education. "We will have to see if she is worthy to live among us at the palace."

"All right." said the king. "But mind you don't harm her."

"No, no. We won't," said the ministers.

They sent a messenger to fetch Miriamu. "You see that mountain," said the Minister for Education. "There is a cross at the top of it. You just have to bring it to us. The king wants it badly, but he can't leave the palace. When you bring it back, then you can marry him."

"All right," said Miriamu.

But Miriamu was very unhappy. The mountain was very high, higher even than Kilimanjaro, and its top was covered with snow. She walked along the beach, kicking the coconuts at her feet. She looked up at the mountain and wept. She knew that the ministers wanted to kill her with their test. They didn't want the king to have any women, because they thought he would neglect his duties if he had any. But Miriamu did not want to disappoint the king, so she started up the mountain.

The first night she thought she would freeze to death. She had on only her school uniform. Already there was much snow on the ground. But then she saw a hut. It had white walls like the palace and a tile roof like her school.

The door of the hut opened. There stood a fierce-looking man. His eyes were flashing on and off, like the signboards of the city. They flashed blue and brown, blue and brown. His hair flashed too, as if there were lightning in it. It flashed yellow and black and red, and sometimes it vanished altogether and the man's skull flashed out at her in different colors. The man had a great bulge in the front of his trousers. It looked like a sack full of snakes. The bulge moved in and out as his eyes flashed. He was a witch, and Miriamu was fearing him very much.

"*Karibu*, Miriamu. Come in out of the snow," said the witch, smiling.

Miriamu was trembling, but she stepped inside. The witch gave her some beer. As she drank, he boasted of all the things he owned and all the things he knew. Miriamu decided to flatter him. What else could she do?

"Your Bata shoes are very smart," she said. "And that suit you're wearing—you must have ordered it all the way from England. I'm sure you are very clever from watching that handsome television. What a beautiful fridge you have–look how it shines!"

The witch was very pleased with her flattery. He continued boasting about all the places he had visited and all the things he knew. Miriamu listened carefully, for she thought he might tell her the secret of how to get to the top of the mountain.

But soon he passed out from drinking too much beer. Miriamu was disappointed. She decided to continue her journey. But when she tried the door, she found that it was locked. All the doors and windows were locked. She could not get out. The house was dark and dirty. She watched the television for a while, and listened carefully to all the programs. But when the national anthem was played and the station shut down for the night, Miriamu had still not learned any useful secrets.

She was hungry. So she went to the fridge and opened it. Then she jumped back. For a *jinni* flew out of the fridge. It was tall and looked like a jellyfish, trailing a cloak of icicles.

"I am the *Jinni* of the Fridge," said the *jinni*. "Ask me a wish, and I shall grant it."

Miriamu was frightened. She began to weep. She told the *jinni* her sad story.

The *jinni* took pity on her, and said: "All right, here is what you must do. When my master wakes, you must give him more beer. Then you must open up his trousers. There you will find a sack of many-colored snakes. You will be fearing them very much, but they will not harm you. Take this tablet, and the snakes will not harm you."

And the *jinni* gave Miriamu an aspirin.

"Take hold of the snakes and push them into all the holes of your body until the snakes are tired and go to sleep. Then my master will be sleepy, as well. Tell him he is very wise. But say that there is one thing you are sure he doesn't know. And that is: how to drive a Land Rover.

"He will say: 'Yes, I know even that!' But you must keep doubting him, until he tells you all the things necessary for driving a Land Rover. Give him more beer. Then he will go to sleep.

"Now, on his watch chain you will find a silver key and a golden key. The silver key is for unlocking the door of his hut, and the golden key is for starting the Land Rover. The Land Rover is in the yard. You can drive it to the top of the mountain and down again. Here is some petrol for you."

And the *jinni* waved his hand. The beer in the fridge turned into tins of petrol.

"Good luck," said the *jinni*. "Now please close the fridge, before I melt like ice cream."

Miriamu did all that she was bidden. After the witch had gone to sleep again, she unlocked the door with the silver key and started up the Land Rover with the golden key. Then she drove the Land Rover to the top of the mountain. The road was very winding, but Miriamu didn't get stuck in any ditch, because she knew all the things necessary for driving a Land Rover.

The cross was high on the highest peak of the

mountain. She drove backwards up to the peak. When the back of the Land Rover hit the rock where the cross stood, the cross fell into the back of the Land Rover. The cross was of gold, and heavier than the heaviest stone. But the Land Rover was very strong. It carried Miriamu and the cross all the way to the bottom of the mountain.

The ministers were surprised to see Miriamu driving along the beach toward the palace. They thought she had died on the mountain. Also, they had never seen a woman driving a Land Rover before. The king was pleased with the cross. He put it in his garden among the palm trees and flowering bushes. The king had many motorcars–Ford Zephyrs and Wolseleys and even a Mercedes. But he didn't have any Land Rover. So he was overjoyed when Miriamu gave it to him."

"The story's not over," Adija said, sitting up in bed. "Where are you going?"

"I'm cold." Salome went to the charcoal brazier where she had warmed her maize-meal supper. She blew on the coals, but got only a face-full of ashes for her trouble; the coals had gone out. The lantern, too, was dimming, and there was no more kerosene. Outside in the street, a woman shrieked. It was the kind of sound a woman makes when a man is teasing her too roughly; at first loud laughter, then a panicky cry. A dog barked. Someone slammed a door. Cursing, Salome took down the army greatcoat she wore when it rained. She spread it over her on the bed. When she offered to share it with Adija, Adija shook her head.

"You're the one who's usually shivering," Salome said.

"As long as I'm awake, the room's warm enough

with the lantern lit." Adija took two cigarettes from her pack, lit them, and handed one to Salome. "You want me to go on with the story?"

"Sure. It's better than freezing in silence."

Adija puffed on her cigarette a few times and then continued:

The king was very pleased with Miriamu and her gifts. "You see, the girl is clever," he said to his ministers. "She is worthy to be my bride. Summon all the chiefs in my kingdom for my wedding!"

"Just a minute," said the Minister for Defense. "*Bado kidogo*, if you please."

The king waited.

The ministers all whispered together. Then the Minister for Education said to the king: "All right, she has brought gifts for you. But what of us? If she doesn't bring gifts for us, we will plot a coup to overthrow you."

"My army is strong," said the king. "I'll take my chances. Let the drummers drum from all the hilltops for my wedding!"

"No, no!" pleaded Miriamu to the king. "They will kill you if we are married now. Let me first get some gifts for them."

"All right," said the king, "But hurry up. I have not had any women for many years, and I am lonely."

Miriamu asked the ministers: "Do you want some lovely Bata shoes and English suits and televisions and fridges? I know where I can get some for you."

The ministers all whispered together again. Then the all shook their heads. "What we want are some pearls from the ocean. Just go to the ocean and fetch some for us," said the Minister for Foreign Affairs.

"But I can't swim," cried Miriamu.

"You don't have to swim," said the Minister for

Transportation. "Just go down to the Nyara Beach Hotel and hire a boat to take you to the reef. On the reef you will find a hole."

"It isn't a very deep hole," said the Minister for Finance, chuckling.

"You can reach in and gather up the pearls," said the Minister for Education. Really, that Minister for Education was the wickedest of the lot. "We will be waiting for you on the verandah."

So Miriamu drove down to the Nyara Beach Hotel in her Land Rover and hired an outrigger canoe. The boatman poled her out to the reef. The ministers waved to her from the verandah. They were laughing as they waved.

Miriamu was weeping with fear, for the water was crashing against the reef. But finally she found the hole. It was a deep, dark hole, not a shallow one as the minister had told her. She was cursing those ministers very much. She knelt down and reached her hand into the hole, though, for she could see the pearls shining up at her our of the water.

As soon as her hand touched the water, something grabbed her. She was pulled down, down into the hole. Seaweeds slid across her face. She thought surely she would drown. But then she got pulled into a cave. There was air in the cave. The air smelled foul and it was dim, but Miriamu could breathe it. She looked around, to see what had pulled her down into the water.

It was an octopus that had pulled her down into the water. It must be a witch thought Miriamu, because it is as strange-looking, in its way, as the man on the mountain. It was black as the underbelly of a cooking pot. Its eyes were full of flames, like the flames that leap out of the end of a rifle. Its arms were very long and strong. At the end of each arm was a weapon. The octopus had knives and spears and *pangas* and rifles and pistols and Sten guns and even bombs. It waved the weapons all at once at Miriamu and its eyes glowed red.

Miriamu was fearing this witch very much. But now she was more clever than before. She told it: "Look how powerful your weapons are! I think that pistol can shoot very straight. That Sten gun, I think it must make a fearsome noise. Can you slice off a man's head with that *panga*? I think so!"

Miriamu was gasping for breath as she spoke, for the octopus was wrapping its arms around her tight. She thought that she would be crushed in the arms of the octopus. But it was pleased that Miriamu was admiring its weapons. It gave Miriamu a small knife to look at.

Now Miriamu remembered what she had learned on the mountain. When the octopus let go of the knife, Miriamu pushed the end of its arm into her vagina. She put another arm into her anus, and another into her mouth and soon weapons were falling all over the floor of the cave. Miriamu was feeling very happy, for the octopus was holding her gently now.

When the last of its arms went limp, the octopus opened its mouth. Inside its mouth was a basket full of shining pearls. Miriamu reached in and took out the basket. She looked down into the basket to admire the pearls. When she looked up, the octopus was gone. In its place was a beautiful woman.

The woman was lying asleep on the floor of the cave. Miriamu rushed to her and woke her. The woman sat up, rubbing her eyes. She was very happy to greet Miriamu.

"*Salaama.*" said the beautiful woman. "Why have you come to this reef?"

Miriamu told her the story of the king and the ministers and the pearls.

"Listen," said the woman. "Those ministers are just going to trick you. I know them. They are the ones who bewitched me into the shape of an octopus many years ago. I will return with you. We will bring my weapons and kill them."

"All right" said Miriamu. "But what if the boatman refuses to carry us?"

"Don't worry. I will give him some pearls," said the woman.

So Miriamu and the woman went back to shore with a boat full of weapons. The ministers were still sitting on the verandah. They were drinking brandy and laughing. But when they saw the boat, they stopped laughing.

As soon as the boat touched the beach, the woman attacked the verandah. The ministers tried to run away, but they were too fat to run fast. The woman threw a bomb and half the ministers were blown up. They lay bleeding all over the verandah.

Then the woman shot all the rest of the ministers with the Sten gun. They were lying on the floor of the verandah. Their organs were splattered on the walls. They were moaning and cursing and clutching their fat bellies. They all bled to death.

The manager of the Nyara Beach Hotel was very unhappy. "What am I going to do with all these dead bodies on my verandah?" he asked.

"Here, take some pearls," said the woman. And the manager was quiet.

Miriamu and the woman drove to the palace in the Land Rover. The people came out into the streets to see them. They were cheering and waving their flags at them. They were happy that the wicked ministers had been killed. Even the palm trees were happy on that day. They were waving their leaves over Miriamu and the woman as the Land Rover drove through the streets of the city.

The king was overjoyed to see Miriamu. He embraced her.

"This is my friend," said Miriamu, and she showed the woman to the king. "She killed all the ministers."

"My ministers are dead?" shouted the king. "*Eii*! This is the best news in many years!" And he greeted the woman in a very friendly way.

"Well, I will be going back to my cave now," said the woman.

"No, no! You must stay!" said the king. "You can come to my wedding. Afterwards you can live in the palace with us. I will make you brigadier of my army."

"All right," said the woman.

The king summoned all the chiefs in the kingdom. He ordered his drummers to drum from all the hilltops for his wedding. He caused the palace to be decorated with flowers of many colors. The sun shone bright on the day of the wedding. As the king and Miriamu walked together into the chapel, the palm trees lifted their leaves toward Heaven.

After the wedding ceremony, the king and his bride had a big party. All the king's friends were there. Queen Elizabeth was there. Elvis Presley was there, and Shashi Kapoor and Pearl Bailey and Miriam Makeba and Pélé and Satchmo and Cliff Richard and the Shadows, and all the famous film stars. Miriamu and the king and the woman sat at the biggest table. They were not drinking beer; they were drinking palm wine and Bee Hive Brandy and Gilbey's

Gin. They were not eating maize-meal porridge, they were eating roasted goat and sheep and prawn curry and coconuts and pawpaw and fish cooked in palm wine. They got very drunk and fat.

Miriamu and the king and the woman stood on the wall of the palace. The people cheered and waved their flags at them. Even the schoolgirls who used to mock Miriamu were cheering. Even the men who used to abuse Miriamu were cheering. Even Miriamu's mother, who used to beat her, was cheering. But now they were cheering only because they were fearing Miriamu.

"Shall I tell the army to chase them away?" the woman asked Miriamu.

"All right." said Miriamu. "Tell the army to chase them into the ocean."

The army chased them into the ocean and they drowned.

Then Miriamu and the king and the woman ate and drank some more. Even the king got drunk. Even Miriamu got fat. Everyone was very happy on that day.

"And that." Adija said, "is the story of Miriamu and the king."

"And the woman." Salome said.

"Yes."

Adija rolled over on her back. Her breasts were flat on her chest, her nipples cold and hard in the chill air. "Was the story good?"

Salome laughed. "I think so. Are you sure you made it up?"

"Of course! You've never heard it before, have you?"

"Yes and no." Salome said. "I have and I haven't."

"Look!" Adija pointed up at the ceiling. A tiny

lizard was running upside down along the corrugated tin. It scurried back and forth, then disappeared under the edge of the roof. "It was gray in that shadow." Adija said. "This afternoon it was orange."

"I don't like lizards. My people say they crawl into your head while you're sleeping and eat your brain."

"I don't believe in witchcraft," Adija said. "I like them."

"You would." Salome shivered. "You're a witch yourself, you know. You've crawled into my brain and now I'm stick with you."

Adija giggled. She pressed her cheek against Salome's broad shoulder and closed her eyes.

Salome let the lantern burn down. As the globe became sooty, the light shrank down the walls, flickering. Still, it seemed to provide some warmth in the room. Light and shadow flickered on Adija's pictures, making the faces indistinguishable, just a wall of glossy squares. Adija pushed closer to Salome beneath the blanket to absorb more of her warmth. Her mouth opened, and soon she was snoring softly.

A car engine roared down the street. Some men shouted and banged on the door of the bar, wanting one last drink. Salome heard them cursing. Tires squealed, the engine roared again. Headlight beams shot through the window, flashed along the walls, then vanished. The smell of dust billowed through the room. Salome reached underneath the bed. Her hand found the handle of her *panga*, and she gripped it tight.

Another car engine approached, this one from the opposite direction. It sounded noisy enough to be a Land Rover, but Salome knew the car, the teacher's tinny old Morris. Footsteps crunched in the dirt outside the room; there was a soft knock on the door.

"What do you want?"

"It's Billy," the voice whispered. "Is Adija there?"

"Adija's sleeping. She is celebrating Independence tonight."

The footsteps crunched in place. "All right. I'll be back tomorrow."

I know you will, Salome thought. You'll all be back. But not tonight.

She pulled the blanket up tighter around Adija's shoulders. Then she lay very still. The shadows flickered down the wall, as if trying to lap up what little warmth was left in the room.

SUPERBALL

Jessie stood in the doorway of the reform school's dining-room, squinting around at the other girls. They were dressed up for the visitors, and she felt scruffy wearing the same t-shirt, frayed jeans, and sneakers that she'd arrived in. When she touched her hair it felt like brittle wires that curled back itchily into her scalp. Her jaw ached from grinding her teeth. So did her mind from trying to decide whether to run or stay.

She wasn't sure if she dared try another runaway. Hitch-hiking, she'd had to fight off a lot of drivers in a lot of states. But if she did get back home, maybe she could talk her mother into keeping her. Give me another chance, Mom, she'd whispered to herself on the bus upstate. She'd never actually gotten around to saying this at home. Her two days between institutions were hazy now, hidden behind a smeared gray mental window through which she viewed her past—and her future, too, the rare times she tried to imagine it. She remembered her mother's slurred voice constantly aimed at her, the feel of the catsup bottle flying out of her hand toward her mother's mouth, and the red explosion it made against the wall. But when she tried to picture her mother—maybe welcoming her in the doorway—all she could see was a blurry image of a TV rerun Mom who always wore a frilly apron and matching smile.

She tried to imagine Richard McClane, her counselor, and Sonia, the staff woman who'd brought her downstairs, as a TV Dad and Mom, but as they walked toward her across the room, the idea seemed stupid. He was old enough but that mustache and crazy necktie somehow disqualified him; she was too beautiful, with her long honey-blond hair and her flowered dress. Jessie looked around at the girls in their clean slacks and blouses and makeup, just standing around talking quietly to each other. Suddenly she stepped up to Richard. "I already had a sandwich. I ain't hungry," she said. "Can I go back upstairs?"

"Everybody's been looking forward to this visit all week," he said, smiling. "You wouldn't want to miss anything."

"The hell I wouldn't."

She tilted away from him, expecting him to yell. But he did something confusing: he leaned over to speak to her; his maroon suit jacket looked soft and woolly close up and smelled like a just-lit cigarette when you're dying for a smoke. "You've just come from home, Jessie," he said quietly. He spoke her name as if he were about to share something confidential with her, and she almost stepped nearer to hear him better. "But most of these girls," he went on, "haven't seen anybody from the outside world in a long time. The ones whose families can't visit them sort of share Peaches' mother and sister today."

Jessie glared straight ahead. "What's that got to do with me? I just got here."

"Well, if you don't join them, the girls'll think that you don't think the visit's important. It'll make them feel bad."

"Oh," Jessie mumbled. She had to look away from his face; she couldn't remember any adult ever focusing on her like that, as if he were sure she'd understand him because she was just as smart as he was. In fact, though part of her did understand him, another part of her thought he was completely off the wall. As soon as he'd turned toward Sonia, too-late questions occurred to her: Why should these girls care about what I think? Why should I give a shit about what they think of me?

Sonia was looking at her. "How do you like the decorations?" she asked.

Jessie shrugged. "It supposed to be Christmas around here?" she asked. Didn't the woman know it was February outside? Red cloths with reindeer prancing on them covered the tables; sprigs of plastic holly were taped around the serving window, framing a view of the huge black kitchen stove and a maze of ventilation pipes.

"I guess the waitresses wanted the place to look especially nice today, and this was all they could find," Sonia said. "It's the thought that counts, though, don't you think?"

"It still looks like a jail," Jessie said. The dining room had a fresh coat of paint—robin's egg blue—but Jessie, who wasn't fooled by paint jobs, could see the outlines of chips in the plaster, probably made by flying plates during a food riot. On the far wall, translucent plastic curtains revealed the steel squares in the windows.

Ronnie, dressed in a white waitress's uniform, strode up to Richard McClane. "How're we going to keep Mr. Paleno out of here today?" she asked in a quiet voice. "If he catch an attitude, it ain't going to look right."

Richard glanced at a door across the rec room with a big ASSISTANT DIRECTOR nameplate on it. "Take a lunch tray into his office. Then he won't have any reason to come out here."

Ronnie nodded and hurried back to the kitchen.

"Thank you," Jessie heard Sonia whisper to Richard.

"I'm going to leave you in charge now," he told her. "But I'll be around."

When he had walked away, Sonia signaled the cook through the serving window and told the girls in the rec room that they could come in. She and Jessie stood in the doorway as they rushed past.

Behind the serving window, a kitchen girl was flipping cheese sandwiches from the grill onto heavy plates arranged in rows along the counter. Ronnie moved around the dining room pouring milk into plastic glasses and telling the girls at each table that if they played around with their food today she'd personally kick their asses. Everyone started eating quietly. The orderliness of the place made Jessie nervous.

She sat down at a table with Sonia and Peaches, who turned her head toward the doorway so often that she hardly ever got a spoonful of soup all the way to her mouth. She looked even more like the movie star in her poster than before, with so much pink and beige makeup on that her eyes looked as if they were peeking through almond-shaped holes in a magazine picture. Even though her tattoos were covered up by a long sleeve, she kept rubbing that arm as she waited. Maybe to distract herself from her nervousness, she began talking with Jessie about her little sister, as if she assumed Jessie would care. Jessie tried not to listen, not wanting to be sucked into anything the way she had been by Mr. McClane.

" . . . I always took Lurleen with me when I worked in the grape arbors after school, just to keep me company," Peaches said. "See, I had to pick grapes or there wouldn't've been no money in the house for food. My mother's so fucking lazy she don't even flush the toilet after herself."

Jessie wrinkled her nose. It was a good thing she wasn't hungry.

"And if I didn't get Lurleen out of the house, and my mother's boyfriend came over—you never knew what that creep'd get up to with us girls."

"My mother's boyfriend was a creep, too." Jessie turned away quickly, ending the conversation, she hoped, by pressing her lips together. She tried not to picture that man coming into her room—a dozen or so more times in two years, until she'd figured out that he probably couldn't kill her any more than he could finish raping her. When she finally got up the nerve to tell the Welfare woman, though, it was in some ways the beginning, not the end, of her troubles. She remembered the smacks she'd gotten in the face from her mother, and being locked out on the front stoop all night. She almost got a mental glimpse of her mother slamming the door, but then she remembered the way the cold cement of the step felt under her ass. It reminded her of other places, like cement park benches in new towns, and the roadside curbs she'd sat on waiting to hitch rides. . . .

"How come your moms is so late, Peaches?" someone asked.

Jessie turned around fast. Now what? A Puerto Rican waitress with flaming red hair was leaning over Peaches, who rolled her eyes and shrugged.

The waitress and another Puerto Rican girl lingered behind Jessie talking in Spanish. Jessie hated it when PRs talked in their secret language like that. They were probably talking about how they could rip her off. She heard the English words "new meat"—meaning her—followed by hushed laughter that made her squeeze her milk glass as if ready to use it for a weapon, which she'd once had to do in another institution. Then the smaller girl, who was called Lucia, said in English, "We wait and see," glancing right at Jessie.

Jessie narrowed her eyes, saying to herself, Don't hold your breath too long waiting. Every fucking new joint she arrived at, she had to prove herself all over again. She was goddamned if she was going to go through it all here—let these bitches think whatever the hell they wanted about her. She glanced around the room until her eyes came to rest on the back of a head of reddish-yellow curly hair—that counselor sitting in the corner in that sharp maroon wool suit. As if he'd overheard what she'd said to herself about the girls, he turned and gave her a wiseass grin. What'd he think, she didn't really mean it? She looked quickly back at Peaches, hoping for more chatter to distract her from feeling as if she were already cracking up in this place.

But then a huge black girl shouted, "Peaches, they're here!" The girls jumped up from their tables and, led by Peaches, made a noisy rush for the doorway. Several stood on chairs to get a better view. Jessie moved away from them to watch.

Peaches walked quickly across the rec room beyond the doorway, her arms outstretched toward her sister. The little girl wriggled out of her mother's grip and ran straight at Peaches. As she rose in the air in Peaches' embrace, she let out a high-pitched squeal that made several of the girls cheer. Even Jessie grinned as Peaches and Lurleen, hand in hand, walked toward the dining-room doorway.

Peaches said almost nothing to her mother, a gaunt woman in canvas shoes, dirty pink socks, and a too-big cotton dress. She kept trying to catch Peaches' eye with a scowl, as if she blamed her daughter for surrounding her with noisy delinquents. Lurleen, though, was perpetually smiling. She had huge, trusting brown eyes, heavy-lidded; her lower lip hung slightly open. She must have been slightly retarded; despite being so small and giggly, she was in fact almost twelve, her age revealed by the tiny bulges—no tinier than mine, Jessie thought—in her pink t-shirt. A lock of whitish blond hair dangled over her forehead; her pale skin seemed to glow in the winter grayness of the room.

Peaches introduced her mother and sister to Sonia and Jessie at her table, and then to the rest of the girls. Her face was flushed from smiling. Jessie sat down gingerly between Sonia and Lurleen, keeping her distance from both.

Waitresses hurried over with bowls of soup and plates of fresh sandwiches. Voices were hushed. All eyes were on Lurleen, who leaned into the crook of Peaches' arm to chew on a sandwich crust.

"Look at that wavy hair!"
"Like a little doll!"

"She's so beautiful!"

Lurleen suddenly fixed her huge eyes on Jessie. Now the little girl was reaching for the leftover sandwich on her plate. For a moment, Jessie froze, going weak inside. She glanced wildly at Peaches, but Peaches was arguing with her mother and didn't hear. Smiling, Jessie slowly pushed the plate closer to Lurleen.

The girl leaned over, her elbow sliding the Christmas tablecloth with it. Jessie caught a glimpse of her bowl of tomato soup tilting off the table. Then she heard a crash. Pieces of heavy china skidded away; jagged red streaks of soup splashed out along the linoleum.

Sonia stood up fast. "It's all right! Please, get back—"

Too late. Several girls rushed toward the splattered soup with napkins. They crowded around, smearing red arcs across the floor their—eyes weren't on what they were doing but on Lurleen.

The streaks of red on the floor—slimy, spreading—made Jessie shudder so hard she had to lean away, doubling over with her hands pressed to her eyes, her fingers gripping the frames of her glasses. Now she could picture her mother—that morning after Jessie had broken a window to get back into the house from the front stoop and had flung the catsup bottle. Her mother stood in the kitchen in her old yellow bathrobe holding the door open for the cops and screaming, Get this kid out of here! She remembered her mother yanking her toward the tallest cop. She remembered digging her fingernails into her mother's wrist, dragging them across the back of her hand as her mother tried to pull free of her. She remembered the smeared blood on her mother's skin and on her own fingers. Then, as the cops yanked her hands behind her and clanked on the cuffs, she went numb, silent. . . .

 Sitting very still at her table, she watched a mop sliding back and forth at her feet. Soon the linoleum was its usual worn, brown color. The room smelled the way dining rooms always smelled: mop water, steam table, sweat. The noises of silverware and girls' voices surrounded her again.

 Was anyone blaming her for the spill? Or blaming Lurleen? Everything was just as before. The floor was clean. Maybe nothing had happened. But from the stricken look on Lurleen's face, Jessie could tell that it had. The girl's mother must have scolded her; now Peaches was arguing with the woman and Lurleen was left alone with her eyes full of tears. Jessie reached for the half sandwich to give her, but it looked so brown and dead on her plate she couldn't stand to touch it.

 She leaned forward, then couldn't think of anything to say. "Don't cry," she finally whispered.

 Lurleen just stared past her as if she hadn't understood. Jessie wiped her own eyes.

* * *

 After lunch, the girls went into the empty rec room. A locked piano had been wedged into one corner; a couch stood in front of a tall brick fireplace. Jessie leaned against a wall midway between the dining room and the couch where the girls were gathered around Lurleen and Peaches. Squatting down in front of the girl, they asked her questions and made funny faces that made her giggle. Jessie, watching, began to smile.

A girl with a huge Afro gave Lurleen a present wrapped in bright Christmas paper. Lurleen tore off the paper and held up a blue rubber ball. It was a superball, the kind that bounces very high and wildly. She threw it down and watched in wonder as it caromed off the floor, off the ceiling, and off a girl's forehead. The girls shrieked and ran after it. Jessie took several steps into the room, then returned to her vantage point by the wall. Following a scuffle near the fireplace, the girls came racing back with the ball.

"Throw it real hard this time!"

"Hey, not at me!"

"Really slam it, Lurleen!

Lurleen did. It ricocheted like a tiny blue rocket around the room. Cheering, the girls dashed off in all directions.

Jessie saw an office door open a crack. Sonia was looking at it, too.

"Calm down!" she shouted suddenly. "It's time for classes!"

Nobody paid her any attention.

The door opened all the way. A man as tall as Richard McClane and much heavier stepped out into the room. His gray hair bristled and his swarthy face was dark red as if he were suffering from a bad headache. Sonia sucked in her breath.

"All right! That's IT!" the man bellowed, his deep voice rolling out into the room. "AT EASE, EVERYONE!"

The girls froze where they were. Jessie flattened herself against the wall. Lurleen ran to Peaches, kicking the Christmas wrapping accidentally so that it fluttered along the floor. The ball kept bouncing. It caromed off a wall and came dribbling across the linoleum toward Jessie. She grabbed it in both hands and held it behind her back.

"Sonia, I hear a lot around here about how the unit staff is supposed to be responsible for their girls," the man said, his voice quieter and resonant with importance. "But when things get out of hand, it's still me that's got to come and calm things down."

Sonia winced. "Nothing was out of control here, Mr. Paleno."

"No? What do you call 'out of control,' then? When they start breaking down the walls?"

"They were not breaking anything!" Sonia's voice cracked. "The girls were just playing. They've got guests."

"I can see that. I haven't gone blind." He gave Peaches' mother a thin smile.

She had been sitting as far back as possible in the corner of the couch. Now she glared out the window across the room. Jessie had seen a look like that before, several times, in Family Court; it said to the judge: I did all I could for this kid—she's all yours now.

"It seems to me," Mr. Paleno continued, "that teaching responsible behavior is still part of our program. At least, I *think* it is." He scratched his head theatrically. "Unless it got thrown out with the rest of the old policies. Did it, Sonia?"

She glanced at the girls who had silently gathered around her. "We're . . . just about to go to classes now, Mr. Paleno. So we'll say good-bye."

"That's fine. But just a moment, please." Mr. Paleno turned slowly to Jessie and smiled down at her. "Now you think I don't know what you've got hidden behind your back, but I do."

"Me?"

"Yes, you." Mr. Paleno's smile vanished. His lips turned gray. "Give it to me. Right now."

Jessie edged along the wall. She started to tremble.

Mr. Paleno held out his hand. "Jessie—you see, I know your name—let's have it."

She squinted up at him. "It ain't your ball!"

Silence. Sonia bit her lip to keep back a smile. The girls jostled each other for good viewing positions.

Jessie glanced around. There was Peaches, who'd talked to her at lunch, and Lurleen huddled against her, her eyes glued to the ball in Jessie's hand. In the dining-room doorway, the tall man with the curly hair was watching her, probably waiting to kick her out if she didn't do what the other man said. Suddenly she didn't want to get kicked out of any more places. Her legs ached; she felt like sitting down in the middle of the floor, sobbing into her lap, letting the ball roll away. But her whole body stiffened against that idea. She took an unsteady step forward, then walked quickly up to Lurleen and held the ball out to her.

Lurleen took it and pressed it against her cheek.

"It's her ball," Jessie said to Mr. Paleno.

Several girls let out their breath. "*Awright!*" someone yelled. Two girls started to cheer but were silenced by a glare from Mr. Paleno.

"Now this," he said, " is pretty stupid."

"It sure is." Sonia stepped beside Jessie, who was staring ferociously up at Mr. Paleno. Several girls began a low muttering.

"Now listen, all of you—" Mr. Paleno was bellowing again, but the girls crowded forward, their voices rising.

"It ain't your ball!"

"Leave that little kid alone!"

Sonia held out her arm to block the girls, then dropped it and stepped out of their way, her eyes bright. The girls pushed past her. Mr. Paleno stepped back into his office, patting the air before him. His voice was drowned out amid the cries from the girls.

"Mean bastard!"

"Honky motherfucker!"

Eventually Sonia and Richard waded into the mob and herded the girls away. Richard and Mr. Paleno went into the office and shut the door.

"Lurleen still got her present!" someone yelled, and a cheer went up. Several girls lifted Jessie's hand and slapped her palm. She got some grins and bumps as Sonia pushed everyone along toward the far doorway.

"You coming with us?" a Puerto Rican girl asked.

Jessie shrugged and walked along with her, but then hung back. Sonia took Peaches' mother into another office to calm her down. Jessie watched the girls shuffle off toward the door, their voices echoing in the big room. She was still flushed from grinning, but the feeling faded quickly as the room emptied.

Seeing the red and green wrapping paper on the floor, she picked it up and began smoothing it out with her fingers. Peaches and Lurleen were still sitting together on the couch. Peaches' gold hair and Lurleen's white face glowed in the dim light. The fireplace behind the couch made a frame around them. They looked like a Christmas card.

Then they, too, got up and left. The room was empty like the inside of a box. Jessie squeezed the wrapping paper into a hard lump in her fist and wandered off toward the dining room. Angry men's voices rumbled behind Mr. Paleno's door. Then the door opened and she heard her name being called. She stopped but didn't turn around.

"Where are you going?"

It was Richard McClane's voice. She let out her breath. He was standing in front of her now, but all she saw of him was his fancy leather boots and the cuffs of his pants.

"You don't got to say nothing to me," she told him, raising her face. "I ain't even unpacked my suitcase." His smile made no sense so she ignored it as best she could. "I ain't sorry for what I did."

"Good," he said, his mustache jumping.

"What?"

"I'm not sorry for what you did either." That confidential tone was back in his voice.

Jessie's eyes rose to the little purple dragons on his necktie; she seemed to be watching a whole flock of them flying past a tie-shaped window. "How come you ain't sorry," she asked. "You don't like that man?"

"Well . . . I was just glad to see Lurleen get her ball back."

"Yeah." Jessie squeezed the wrapping paper between her fingers.

"I think you ought to unpack," he said. "You can stay."

"I can?"

"If you want to."

She stared past him and the dragons at the wall, and stopped smiling. "It don't make me no nevermind," she said. "I ain't got noplace else to be."

Then, stuffing the bright wad of paper deep into her pocket, she walked toward the door where the other girls had gone.

THE OASIS

Was it a mirage, that bank? It floated before him on waves of heat, a low rectangular building whose walls were the same lonely color as the African desert behind it. Pulling his check from his briefcase, Alain Mercier hurried across the village square toward its open door. Some French Legionnaires watched him from the steps of their barracks. In the shadow of an ancient mud-brick mosque, old men in tattered *djelebias* followed him with their eyes as he vanished into the building.

Inside, he took a deep breath of delicious shade. On the wall, gecko lizards darted across a framed photograph of the premiere of France. The bank was amazingly cool. He thought he noticed the scent of fresh rain—though no rain had fallen here for several weeks.

He blinked. Behind the counter, in a pool of light where incandescent dust motes swirled down from the window, sat the most beautiful woman he had ever seen.

He was a heavy, shy young man, smooth-faced and blue-eyed, and though he had come to this region a year ago to learn about its people, he was still without much personal experience of beautiful women. Setting down his briefcase, he strode up to the bare counter and thrust his check toward the teller.

She had just begun painting her nails with a tiny brush, and appeared to take no notice of him. He watched her moving fingers, feeling the sweat run beneath his stiff khaki shirt. She inspected the red nail of her right forefinger, then replaced the brush in its little bottle. Her eyes were black pearls. Her face shone a deep, dark mahogany, the color of the spirit masks he had seen dancers wear.

Suddenly she smiled up at him. "Welcome," she said in Bambara.

The check fluttered out of his fingers. He trapped it against the counter. "Thank you. I only wish. . . ." He was trying to speak in her language. ". . . make paper here become cash."

Her gaze was a soft breeze against his face. "You may sign the check, then," she said, and arched her fingers, palm up, toward an antique pen and inkwell.

As he wrote his name, he couldn't get a good grip on the pen; his signature looked not his own. He put the check down and stepped back, digging his fingers into his thick, brown hair.

"You have come far, monsieur," she said. Her white teeth sparkled like cowrie shells. She did not even glance at the check.

"Far. Yes." And suddenly he realized how very tired he was. "I have so many places to go, things to do—" He waved his hand toward the north, though now, indoors, he could no longer be sure of his sense of direction. He tried to picture the track that wound like an ancient river bed across the Sahara to Tomboktou, his destination.

"You can rest here." She picked up her nail brush again.

He sat on the bench against the wall, facing her across a space of only a few meters. For something to do while he waited, he made a mental field map of the bank: two rooms—this one, and, behind the counter, a deeper room divided into empty wire teller's cages that might have gone on forever into the shadowy darkness. He was evidently the bank's only customer. Opening his briefcase, he tried to read his papers.

Each time the woman moved even a little, he was distracted as if splashes of color were dancing in his peripheral vision. The robe that flowed around her slim body was an aqueous blue; the shapes of her small pointed breasts tilted down like fish watching her hands at work. Her cheeks were so smooth that he was sure he knew how they would feel against his palm, though he had never touched anything as cool and soft in his life.

His check was now resting on a French instruction book he hadn't noticed before. Removing his pocket watch, he leaned forward. "Madame, is problem about check?"

Her nail brush stopped in mid-air. "I am not 'madame,'" she said. Practicing her French, he supposed; it was nearly as bad as his Bambara. "Myself: 'mademoiselle.'—not married." She pointed to her ears whose bare lobes peeked out from beneath her kerchief, and he recalled that in this region, when a woman married, she was given enormous gold earrings to wear—the couple's savings account.

"Ah." He nodded. "And the check?"

"Only the cashier can encash it." Her eyes flicked nervously down to the far end of the counter where a skeletal cage stood, its circular steel mouth waiting. "But first, the clerk must approve it."

He opened the watch in his hand. It seemed to have stopped. "And when do you think the clerk might come?"

The woman applied her brush to another nail. His question floated on the dust motes between them until it became a memory.

Turning toward the door, he watched a boy slowly leading a camel along the dirt path that led away from the square. Then, in what seemed seconds but surely must have been longer, the two figures reappeared as dots on the horizon. A gust of sand obliterated everything from his view. He raised his hands to shield his eyes, but neither the sand nor the heat blew into the bank.

"Monsieur Mercier, would you like coffee?" Her voice resonated like the sound of a *kora*, an African harp.

He was thirsty, and also strangely hungry. "You're very kind."

"Not kind. It's good to have company. One is too much alone—you understand?"

He stared at her. Now that he was no longer in constant motion—conducting interviews, taking notes—he did understand. "Yes," he said.

She smiled back. When she rose from her stool, her green cotton dress rippled down her body all the way to her ankles. First she brought him a bowl of cool water for washing, then a cup of coffee. He watched her stir it, her hand circling slowly above the steaming cup. He could not have said how long he'd stood gazing into the little whirlpool of dark liquid. Then the spoon was gone; the surface of the coffee was still. He drank it down. It was both bitter and saturated with a perfumed sweetness.

When he finally raised his face, he saw that three fingernails of her right hand were now a gleaming crimson. "Pardon me for mentioning it, Mademoiselle Touré," he said, "but I'd like to know about the check."

Her lower lip pouted out. She put down her brush. "The clerk who must approve the check, he has gone to the market to buy medicines for his aunt. She has taken sick."

"Ah. I'm sorry to hear it." He returned to the bench with his cup. It was full again. As he took a sip from it, he noticed that the hunger he had felt before was gone, replaced by a new, pleasanter kind of expectancy. He began to organize his fieldwork into chapters. It was fortunate that he had brought all his data with him. The cycles of birth and death, the sensuous rituals of courtship and marriage he had observed—all were coming to life for him now.

When he looked up again, someone had moved his check to another desk. It had acquired a thin layer of dust.

"Mademoiselle Touré, did the clerk come back?" he asked.

"He was here briefly. It's very sad—he had to go to his aunt's funeral." She fingered the shiny metal cross at her neck. Her plump, round bosom heaved. "If you must know, Alain, he approved the check before he left. Now the deputy assistant manager must sign it."

"Does the deputy assistant manager also have trouble in his family?"

"No, no. It's a joyous day for him." Her French

was remarkably good. "Today his son is to marry the girl he's been courting."

"The boy's very fortunate," Alain said. Sitting back in his chair, he lost himself in his work again.

"What are those papers you're always writing?" she asked.

"As a matter of fact, Fanta," he said, "this chapter's on courtship customs."

Smoothing her short, pink skirt over her lap, she flashed him a sideways look that made his cheeks flush. "You've done your research well, haven't you?"

"I've been inspired recently." He grinned.

Humming, she lifted the hinged flap in the counter and set down a plate of rice and fried plantain before him. Like all her dishes, it was delicious, yet not fattening; he ran his hand down his freshly laundered cotton shirt, feeling the flatness of his belly.

"I like to read these." Fanta pointed with her nail brush to the newspapers on the counter. "Will you be getting more of them?"

Alain could not recall where they had come from. Perhaps one of the French legionnaires had given them to him. But now the only soldiers he saw outside were Africans in baggy uniforms.

"I'll try to order some in the mail," he said. "By the way, have you heard from the deputy assistant manager?"

"Yes, he's gone on leave. His son's wife has given birth to a little boy." The wistful expression on her face made Alain glance away. "Before he left, though, he passed the check on to the assistant manager."

"And where is he?"

She planted her hands on her hips. "Why are you so impatient?"

"You've got to understand, I have plans—so many things to do!"

"Of course." She rolled her eyes.

He turned away from her. He could see that his check had been moved from the desk to her left to a desk directly behind her. It seemed to be making its way in a semi-circle; the last stop would be the cashier's cage beside the door where the sun's glare was burning a yellow stripe in the floor. He watched a man drive a tractor across the square toward a petrol pump that wobbled like a flame in the heat. Inside the bank, though, the air was still cool. Several geckos darted on the wall around the framed picture of the republic's new president, a distinguished-looking black man in a gray suit and tie.

Alain returned to his work, steadily filling his thick pads of paper. He wrote "Volume Two" at the top of the page. What had happened to Volume One? He recalled that Fanta had proofread it and mailed it off.

"The Anthropological Institute was very complimentary," she said. Her heavy earrings swung beside her neck like golden conch shells.

"The work went better than I could have imagined," Alain said. "It's a shame we won't be paid more for publication."

"We've enough to get along."

"But for how long?"

She smiled. "Long enough."

"I hope you're right," he said.

For a while, he wrote steadily and she worked on her nails. Then, thinking that he heard some movement from the far end of the room, he looked up from his papers. His wife turned back toward him on her stool. Her forehead was clenched as if she had just been shouting at someone in the shadowy space behind her.

"Was that the assistant manager?" he asked.

"Yes. But he has gone." Her face was still clouded over. "He left the check for the manager."

"The manager...." Alain gazed out the door. Women were setting up vegetable stalls against the barracks wall across the newly tarmacked square. He heard an amplified call to prayer from the mosque whose gleaming white minaret rose above the busy streets of the city.

"You still ask about that check." She moved her mirror to inspect her hair, which she had braided in elegant cornrows. "Aren't you content with me, Alain?"

"Of course!" he said, and was glad to see her pouting expression fade. "We mustn't fight, dear," he added.

"Especially not now." She rested her hand on her belly.

He walked to the doorway, holding his fingers out to catch some drops of water. The rains had been especially good, and the garden was thriving. The bright red flowers Fanta had planted just outside glistened with moisture. Smiling, Alain watched her pick up her brush; she had completed all the nails of her right hand and was now starting on the left one. He returned to his work, and became so absorbed in it that he did not glance up until he heard a small cry from behind the counter.

Lifting the baby in her arms, Fanta unbuttoned her blouse to free a heavy brown breast. The child began to suckle. "How I'll miss this when he begins to eat porridge," she said.

"We can't put it off much longer," Alain said, smiling.

"Horny goat!" She laughed.

Local custom forbade a man from approaching his wife for several years while her infant was nursing. Alain's joy at returning to her, however, was gradually diminished by worry: how would they afford school fees for little Benoit-Seku? Fanta's gold savings would not support them forever. He squinted into the murky space behind her, and saw that his check had been moved to another desk.

"It's turned yellow at the edges," he said.

The lines deepened in Fanta's forehead. "The manager said he'll try to get approval for encashment when he goes to the capital," she said, her voice flat. She was speaking Bambara again; it was not safe to speak French in the republic now. "But the roads are so dangerous these days!" She glanced up at the photo of the scowling general on the wall. Geckos no longer played around its frame.

Alain unfolded the newspaper on his desk. "The garrison from Tomboktou has been called in," he said in her language. He was fluent in it now.

"Seku's school will be closed. Next they'll be drafting him into the army."

"No, he was talking of joining the rebels, don't you remember?"

"Let's hope so." For luck, she touched the tiny leather bag of Koranic verses that rested on her round bosom. Its cord was all but invisible in the folds of her flesh.

The sand blew past the doorway and drifted toward the barracks. An old man led a camel past a charred petrol pump. Bricks from the bombed-out shops still littered the square, but all was quiet now. Alain wrote slowly. After a while, he dozed, his head on his stack of papers, his fingers resting in his thinning gray hair.

He saw or dreamed that he saw a bony figure move into the cashier's cage as if stepping out of a dark haze of cobwebs. Waking suddenly, Alain was sure he heard footsteps—and paper being rustled, rustled.... But as before, the wire cage was empty. He leaned forward, the cords in his neck stretching beneath his beard.

"Fanta, was that the manager?"

Her nail brush stopped in mid-air.

"It was him, wasn't it?" he asked.

"Yes." She shifted her wide hips on her stool. "But Alain, there was mail today. Seku-Ali's commission has come through. He'll have a big salary now!"

"I wonder if he'll help us."

"Of course he will. He's a good young man. Don't you remember how he used to work with us in the garden?"

"I remember that year we tried planting yams...."

"It was your idea."

"The boy kept asking for them."

"Yes, and you rescued two and watered them every day."

"There were at least half a dozen."

She laughed. "All right, three. One for each of us."

"At any rate, there were enough," he said.

"It's true." She touched his arm. "There were."

"But this year," His gazed out the door at the expanse of sand and the fiery sky above it. "The drought...."

"It's never been so dry." She shook her head slowly, and her stretched empty earlobes swung against her neck. How worried she must be, he thought, more than she shows. He rose, his joints creaking, and lay his hand over hers.

"Careful—my nails!" She waved her fingers in the air to dry them. The sleeves of her long black *burqa* shook along the sagging flesh of her arm. Four nails of her left hand were now bright red.

He paced across the room and stopped before the doorway. Outside, a caravan made its way along the highway. Tombstone-sized slabs of salt were strapped to the camels' humps. He sniffed the air, searching for a remembered scent.

When he returned to the counter, Fanta was tearing open another envelope. "It's from the Ministry of Defense!"

"From Seku-Ali?"

"Yes! He's going to mail a money order, just as he promised!"

Alain held up the letter, squinting through his spectacles. The floor seemed to tilt and right itself beneath his feet. From the frame on the wall, the young president smiled down on the letter in his hands.

"We can forget about cashing the check now!" Alain said. In fact, he had not thought of it in a very long time, and did so now with reluctance, even dread. "Can't we, Fanta?" he asked.

She had twisted around to face the darkness behind the cashier's cage. Now she turned slowly back to him. Tiny white corkscrews stood up in the brushed mat of her hair. "Ah, if only we could!" she said.

He pressed his knuckles against his lips.

"The cashier—the manager has given him the

key to the cash drawer," she said, her eyes cast down at her fingertips. "He'll be here soon."

"But . . . can't we delay him a little longer?"

She shut her eyes tight.

Frowning, Alain took out his watch. But of course it was still stopped. What good would it have done to look at it anyway? He flung the watch to the floor. It skidded past the cashier's cage and cracked against the frame of the blazing doorway.

"You mustn't tire yourself like that," Fanta said.

"The damned man can take back his money—" A gust of hot wind choked off his voice.

She began to paint the last nail of her left hand.

"Wait!" He wanted to protest that he needed time to finish his book, but he saw that the briefcase beside his desk was not only empty but full of cobwebs. Hot sand was blowing through the door and swirling all over the room. It felt gritty between his teeth and burned in his eyes. What had happened to all his plans? They blurred like a mirage on the horizon behind him. "Strange—that I could have thought them so important," he said.

"Thought what?" she asked.

"The things I was going to do."

"Ah." Her eyes danced. "Those."

"But I remember other things. . . ." He smiled. "Plantains, yams."

Fanta screwed the cap on the little bottle. Now her cheeks were damp with tears. She brushed them away. "It's time," she said.

He sighed, his skinny arms dangling from his tattered *djelebia*.

"Will you help me, Alain?"

He straightened his back. How dazzling her smile

is, he thought, her teeth still white as cowrie shells.

"Of course, dear," he said.

He lifted the hinged flap in the counter for her. She took his hand as she stepped through. Side by side, they moved across the floor toward the cashier's cage. The glare of the sun had turned it to molten wire. They felt, rather than saw, the movement of the figure inside. Shuddering, they heard the rustling of paper, and held each other's gaze.

The bank went silent. For a long moment the sand stopped blowing. Then the breeze came up again, and it was cool, and smelled to them like rain.

NIGHT OWL

In my dream, I want to warn Father Taggart, but I get so snarled in people's scarves and mufflers in the church vestibule that I can't reach him. Cackling, another priest pokes a finger into his eye. The parishioners smile as Father Taggart staggers backwards, blood dribbling down one cheek like red tears.

Beside the church is a cliff where a gang of boys stand in a semi-circle around him. We all watch him lose his footing and fall. In mid-air, he turns into a bristly black owl, wings flapping as he struggles to rise.

I lift my tennis racket for an overhead slam. Whack!—a clump of feathers plummets back down and vanishes into the air. The boys cheer. As I release my grip on the racket's handle, it peels the skin away from my palm.

* * *

Going to the Episcopal church every week was my family's only ritual. We would have a big breakfast on Sunday morning and then I'd get dressed up in itchy flannel slacks, a blazer, and a striped tie that my father tightened against my windpipe as we stood before the hall mirror. He picked invisible specks of lint from his suit. My mother tugged her jacket down over her stomach, stretching the buttons.

"I always look so dowdy!" she said and hurried back upstairs. She'd stopped drinking recently and was often nervous. When she finally got into the car, she'd changed her hat and suit. My father looked at his watch and gunned the engine; gravel rattled under the floor.

I liked some of the Bible stories, but the rest of the services drifted past me. I usually dozed through the sermons—until a new priest, Father Taggart, became the assistant minister. His slide-guitar voice reminded me of the Night Owl, a disc jockey on the country radio station I listened to under the covers after bedtime. He looked like a former football player; I liked the way he walked with his shoulders rolling forward as if about to carry the ball in for a touchdown. His awkward movements concealed a limp. Beneath his cassock he wore big brown shoes that were always scuffed; my father often remarked on this. His eyebrows met over the bridge of his nose, which inspired the boys to call him "monster-man." I didn't think of him that way—I never intended to torment him at all.

The first time I heard him preach, he said that Jesus could be a two-fisted man of action when he needed to be; he wasn't always "nice." Remember the time he overturned the money-changers' tables in the temple? I did. I pictured myself rampaging through the parish-house bazaar snapping a six-foot Lash LaRue rawhide special. I flicked jars full of quarters to the floor and splattered homemade cakes against the walls. My parents, whose cocktail party guests were always telling them what a nice boy I was, gazed in horror at the debris, their faces ravaged by frosting.

On my way out of church, I grinned at Father Taggart as I shook his hand. From the roughness of his grip, I could tell that he could spot a fellow man of action, despite the slacks-and-blazer costume that the man's parents made him wear.

Sermons about overturning money-changers' tables, or about how much easier it was for a camel to pass through the eye of a needle than for a rich man to enter Heaven, weren't popular with a congregation whose members included many of Wall Street's top corporate executives. My father preferred the sermons of the regular minister, Father Osgood, who preached in liturgical tones about the servant who increased his master's holdings manyfold instead of leaving them, so to speak, in low interest-bearing accounts. Father Osgood was a plump little man with cobwebby hair and the expression of someone perpetually holding back a sneeze. My mother once called him a fussy old woman, which delighted me, but not my father.

"I suppose you prefer the new man," he said as we drove back from church. "All the women like the way he limps around like a wounded buffalo."

"That's a very unfair thing to say." My mother glared out the car window. "Anyway, it was your vestry that hired Father Taggart."

"No, it wasn't. The bishop pressured Father Osgood into taking him on without consulting us."

"I suppose you've decided to get rid of him, then." She sighed.

"We have to see if he's up to doing his job, first."

"He hardly ever gets a chance to do anything but follow Osgood around the altar."

"Oh, he'll get plenty to do, don't worry."

"Like what?"

"Christ, Marian!" My father jammed on his brakes at a stoplight. I held on to the armrest in the back seat. "You don't know anything about how organizations work. If you can't say something constructive—"

I leaned over the seat. "Do you like Father Taggart?" I asked her.

"I don't know," she said, pressing her fingers against her forehead. "I don't know anything."

* * *

It was announced from the pulpit that the seventh graders were to start confirmation instruction, but I wasn't sure that I wanted to become a member of the church. Once I joined up, I might never be able to get out. The new priest's sermons had started me thinking about religion, and now I wasn't certain that I believed everything that I'd been hearing about it for years. When I told my father I wanted to think things over before starting confirmation classes, he turned away from the papers on his desk and frowned down at me.

It had nothing to do with believing things or not, he said. Joining the church was a responsibility I had as a member of the community, just as serving on the board of vestrymen was his responsibility. He didn't intend to let me make a spectacle of myself by trying to be different. "And don't upset your mother about this business, either," he said, "You know how hysterical she can get."

I couldn't resist talking to her, though. "Oh, *please* don't go against your father on this!" she said, her voice rising. "You know how he always takes it out on me when things go wrong."

I kept my mouth shut for the time being.

* * *

It was strange being in church on weekday afternoons. Rows of empty pews faced a high-roofed cavern where the altar, in shadow now, was surrounded by a low communion rail. A smell of old burnt wax candles hung in the air. Sitting with my confirmation class in the front pews, I gazed up at the sunbeams that flowed through the windows and imagined myself swimming upstream on the sparkling dust motes, through the bright Bible pictures, and outdoors into the sky.

The boys in the class (the girls were being taught on another day) were all from Country Day, the private school where I'd just started that fall. On the first afternoon, we waited noisily for a priest to arrive. The boys' mocking jokes made me feel a little more at ease with them. But when I saw Father Taggart walk in from the side door, I quieted down. I'd never seen him wearing anything but a cassock; today he had on black pants and a flannel shirt, as if he'd been hiking in the woods. His long face wore a tired expression; his eyes were strangely red-rimmed behind his glasses. He carried a stack of glossy blue booklets under his arm. From the off-balance way he stood looking at us, I was sure this was the first class he'd been assigned to teach.

He cleared his throat. "Hi, boys," he said.

"Hahy. Hahy." Several kids were amused by his twangy accent, but I liked it.

He tried to grin, but at the same time he wanted to look stern like someone in charge. Moving with a lurching motion, he handed out the booklets. "This book here's called the Holy Catechism," he said.

"What's it about, Father?" A crew-cut boy in the front pew put mock-eagerness into his voice.

"I hoped I could use some other books, but Father Osgood wanted these. Anyhow—" He looked wearily down at the blue booklets. "These are a bunch of questions and answers about the church. You'll have to—well, I'll help y'all memorize them."

"*Memorize?*" Groans went up.

Father Taggart clenched his fists at his sides. "Wait, I'll go get my attendance sheet." He turned and went out the side door.

"Look at him stagger," a boy whispered.

"My father says he drinks," someone else said.

"No, it's from an old football injury," I said, making it up.

"My father says he's a commie," another boy said.

"He's just a flunky for old Osgood."

"No wonder his wife took off. You should have seen her—what a hillbilly!"

When Father Taggart returned, he did his best to explain the deadly catechism booklet.

Now his voice sounded like a guitar string that kept going flat no matter how hard you tried to tune it. Over the next weeks, he struggled to keep our attention by organizing memorization contests, but nobody cared about winning them. I actually tried to remember some answers, but when Father Taggart called on me, I stammered something that was so wrong it was funny—or at lease my new schoolmates thought so. Smoldering, I blamed the priest for their laughter, though he looked as disturbed as I did.

After this, one boy intentionally garbled answers and the others pretended to persecute him with derisive laughter. This reduced him to fake tears and prompted Father Taggart to intervene. "Let's have a little compassion here, dammit!" he would roar. Every time it happened, I got more and more frustrated that he never caught on to the game. Sometimes I joined in the laughter. Having started, it couldn't stop. One day, Father Taggart asked to see me about this after class.

We walked through the church basement ducking grimy steam pipes, our footsteps echoing in the dim corridors. Despite the thumping of the nearby furnace, his office was chilly; he wrapped a long scarf around his neck before he sat down and pointed to an old armchair for me.

"I didn't mean to make so much noise." I told him.

He stared at me, his big round jaw set tight. "Okay," he said. "But what's troubling you, Jerry?"

I glanced around. The office was about a quarter of the size of my father's office in New York, with no windows or oil paintings or carpet. Over the old wooden desk, a magazine photo was taped to the wall: a mountain landscape with orange foliage, maybe the place where Father Taggart came from. "That catechism booklet doesn't make any sense to me," I said.

He sighed. "I can see that." His drawl had a gentle cadence to it; the heavy glasses he wore gave him an owlish look. "But you're not sure you want to be confirmed at all, are you?"

I sat up. "How did you know?"

"It shows in your eyes."

"Really?" No one had ever looked that closely at me before.

He smiled, and I could see that his teeth were crooked. "Having doubts is okay—did you know that?"

"I guess not."

"Well, we all have them."

"Oh," I said. I pulled my windbreaker tighter around my throat. It was cold in here, though the picture over his desk seemed to be trying to give off some light like a recessed box of flames. "Why do people have to join a church, anyway?" I asked finally.

He gazed at the wall beside me as if he were trying to read words too faint to make out. "Well, to find a haven where you won't be alone and folks'll always care about you no matter what, like a family. Everybody's got to have someplace to *belong*." His voice was on-key now and twanging with a resonance I'd never heard before. He leaned forward in his chair; I could smell his sweat. His scarf ends dangled down around his knees like rope. "There's supposed to be a communion with other people. Folks need that worse'n they know. To exist completely *outside*—well, that's hell."

"But what if you can't help it? I mean, being outside?"

His smile faded. The furnace pipes thudded out in the corridor. "I don't know," he said finally. He took a pack of cigarettes from a desk drawer and lit one. I'd never seen a priest smoke before. He used a small tin can for an ashtray. "But I'm sure your confirmation means a lot to your father. I wish I knew more about your family. Is anyone else in it religious?"

I thought about this. "My father isn't really religious. My mother's not, either," I said. "But I think my grandfather was. When he was in a hospital, he kept preaching to people...." I stopped. This wasn't something I was ever supposed to talk about. I'd overheard my father say once that in the hospital they'd taken away his father's shoelaces and belt and watched him every minute.

The priest drew hard on his cigarette. Smoke drifted toward the ceiling. "Do you think," he asked, "that unless somebody's got the kind of faith your grandfather did, he hadn't ought to join a church?"

"Yeah, that could be." I nodded. "Do you think I should quit the class?"

"You know, Jerry, I believe you'll feel better if you could speak with your father the way you did with me. He might understand." Looking me in the eye, he nodded his crooked-toothed smile at me.

Just then, because I suddenly trusted him, I believed it, too.

* * *

That night I knocked on my father's door while he was working at his desk. The catechism booklet was rolled up in my back pocket. Usually I tried to keep from putting my full weight down on the carpet when I was in my father's room, but this time I strode straight to the chair beside his desk and sat down.

"I was talking to Father Taggart today about, you know, the confirmation...."

He stopped writing and turned to me. Above his half glasses lines shot up his forehead. "Why?"

I glanced away. "I was just sort of talking with him."

"It won't work with me, son." He lay his gold pencil on his ledger.

My chair seemed to shift beneath me as if it were suddenly resting on jelly. "What?"

"If you think you're going to get out of your responsibility—even if this Father Taggart says you can—you're wrong."

"He didn't say that. He just said I should talk to you."

I felt a tightness in my throat. My nose was running. I couldn't think straight. I tried to start over, but I could hear the futility in my voice. "There's things about the church I don't understand—"

"That's what we're paying that priest to teach you." My father's voice was deep and clear. He never took his eyes off me for an instant. "If that man's not doing his job—"

"He is! But all we do is memorize this stupid booklet." I hated the whininess in my voice. It wasn't just the catechism I'd wanted to talk about, but I'd already pulled it from my pocket.

He glanced down at the cover. "Listen, Jerrett, you just get through it and move on. You don't fuss about a job of work that's set before you."

I clenched my fists. "I'm not fussing!"

"Sounds like it to me. Wipe your nose, for crying out loud."

I did, turning away. Then I wobbled out of the room with my wrist wet with snot.

In my room, I paced and paced. *You'll feel better,* Father Taggart had said. How the hell could I have believed that? I attacked his booklet with both hands. It was tougher than it looked. I cut my fingers on the staples as I broke its spine.

* * *

"You become a member of the church at the moment you take your first communion." Father Taggart told us a week later. By then I knew that the only way I could avoid this fate was to get kicked out of the confirmation class. I had no idea how to accomplish this—until Father Taggart started talking about the meaning of holy communion. For years, I'd watched Father Osgood put wafers into people's mouths and give them sips of wine from a fancy silver goblet. When people drifted slowly back from the altar rail afterwards, their faces looked sleepy and preoccupied, as if they were breathing a perfumed haze that only adults could smell. I asked my parents after church what had been going on at the altar but they told me I'd learn about it when I was confirmed.

Now Father Taggart was telling us the secret: according to the church, the snack at the altar rail was the body and blood of Jesus. I'd heard this before but had dismissed it as being too gruesome and farfetched to believe. Did my parents believe this cannibal story? I couldn't imagine that they did. Did Father Taggart think it was true? He couldn't! Then how could he be trying to get me to go along with it? I was even more furious with him.

"Why are you telling me I have to eat Jesus?" I suddenly asked from the front pew.

Father Taggart stepped backwards. All whispering around me stopped.

"What part of Jesus's body do people get those wafers from, anyway?" I demanded, my voice rising. "Are they pieces of skin? Or eyelids? Or do people cut slices off his leg like it was a drumstick or something?" I felt a grimace stretching my face. "Do people suck the blood out of him with a syringe, like when you get a blood test?"

Pandemonium. Boys made retching sounds. They clutched their mouths with cupped hands. They leaned over sideways into the aisle holding their stomachs. The church echoed with laughter.

Father Taggart pounded on the pew rail with his catechism book to quiet everyone down. He glared at me as he spoke; sweat trickling down his temples. The booklet swung limply from his hand, its cover in tatters. He was trying to explain about communion and the symbolism of the sacrifice or sacrament or something, but all around me boys were tearing off invisible pieces of flesh with their teeth, and pretending to shoot each other with spurts of blood from the crooks of their arms. I stared at the floor. The laughter echoed to the rafters.

When I looked up again, Father Taggart was gone. The front of the church was empty. I rubbed my eyes.

"Where'd he go?" I asked the boy sitting next to me.

The boy pointed to the side door near the altar. "He looked like he'd been whacked in the face." The boy laughed.

"Great question," someone said to me. But I didn't feel very great.

We waited. The church stayed quiet.

"He can't just leave us here," somebody said.

"He has to get us confirmed."

"Yeah, it's what he's getting paid for."

I squashed down in my seat.

Several boys shouted in unison, "Forgive us our trespasses!"

"We're sorry, Father Taggart!" someone called in a sing-song voice.

More laughter, but it quickly died.
"Come on back, Father!"
"He doesn't give a damn about us, the bastard."
"Monster-man!"
"Shit, what're we going to do now?"
Finally I walked out through the side door to look for him. The corridor beneath the church smelled of sweat and furnace oil. Father Taggart' office door was ajar. I walked up to it and stopped. He was sitting with his back to me, his feet up on his desk as if he were sighting between his shoes at the photograph of autumn-colored mountains. The room was full of cigarette smoke. His hand moved. He raised a small brown bottle from the desk to his mouth, and his head titled back at a crazy angle. I hurried away.

* * *

On confirmation Sunday, I arrived at church in a new Brooks Brothers suit. Father Osgood was to give the class a quiz on the catechism. I planned to fail it. The elderly priest sailed out of the side door toward the front pews, his round belly riding high in his floor-length cassock. Father Taggart, in black pants and collarless shirt, limped out after him and stood against the wall.

"Well, Father Taggart, is the class ready to be confirmed?" The old priest's tone was jocular; the question's answer was meant to be automatic.

I heard no answer, and turned around in my seat. Father Taggart frowned, his brows meeting in the middle.

"Father Taggart, the bishop is going to arrive at any minute now. We can't let him down."

"The boys don't know the catechism," Father Taggart said in a weary voice.

Father Osgood pinched the bridge of his nose. "Didn't you teach them?"

"I did my best," he said, "But it wasn't enough."

"Well, we'll see." Father Osgood glided closer to the front row of pews on invisible feet.

"Now who can tell me—" He gave us a thin, patient smile. "What is the duty of all Christians?"

Silence. The boys looked down, sideways, everywhere but at the priest's face. He asked some more catechism questions in his high voice, then, getting no answers, turned to Father Taggart. "I must say, this is simply atrocious."

"I know it is." Father Taggart stared at his scuffed shoes.

"Never mind. There are other ways of finding out what Episcopalians are required to know." He turned to the boy beside me. "What is the name of the town where Jesus was born?"

"Bethlehem," the boy said, glancing away.

"That's right. That's good."

"Wait a minute!" Father Taggart lurched down the aisle. "That wasn't in the booklet! You told me they had to memorize the damn thing!"

"Uh, shall we have a word together?" Father Osgood took Father Taggart by the arm and guided him out the side door. I could see them talking in the corridor. The old priest pointed a long finger at the young priest's face.

"You all set me up!" Father Taggart shouted. He turned on his heels, an awkward movement for him. His shoes made clumping sounds down the hall. I had the impulse to run after him but I was hemmed into the pew, and then the organ started to play.

Adults were filing the pews behind us. Father Osgood came back alone, his face crimson. He asked us a few hurried, easy questions from the Bible. I wouldn't answer the one he put to me, but he just went on to the next kid, who did answer it, smiling.

"Well done, boys," he said, and sailed up the aisle as the bishop stepped through the door.

The soft organ music filled the air like a pastel fog. The service began. I knelt with the other boys. The Bishop of Connecticut, a small man with wavy hair and purple robes that smelled of dry cleaning, rested his hand on my hair. A chilly sensation spread over my scalp as if he were breaking an egg there.

"We receive you into the holy fellowship. . . ." he told us.

The boys raised their heads one by one, blinking. I walked up the aisle, my eyes on the carpet, to sit with my parents. My mother smiled at me through her hat-veil. My father leaned toward me and gave me a nod.

People began shuffling toward the altar to receive communion. I stepped out of the pew, letting my mother go ahead of me, then my father. I took a few steps. Then I stopped. Fathers, mothers, the boys from my class, passed in front of me, but I didn't move. In a few minutes, the first of the communicants began to file back up the aisle. A cloud of holiness seemed to have settled over them. Their lips were pressed lightly together as if they were all humming the same note, one I couldn't hear. Even the boys in my class looked transformed, pious, miraculously turned into copies of their fathers.

The aisle was crowded with families coming and going. My mother, then my father, slid back into the pew. I sat down beside my mother. Her eyes were closed; she didn't see me. My father's eyes were open. And he didn't see me either.

Father Taggart did. As Father Osgood served someone from a silver goblet, Father Taggart followed behind him, holding a wine decanter in both hands like a football he wanted to lateral. He stopped, his shoulders rolled forward awkwardly, and his eyes met mine. I expected an angry glare from him, but on his face was the loneliest look I'd ever seen.

After the service, I pushed through the crowd outdoors searching for him, though I had no idea what I'd say. I couldn't find him. My parents' friends blocked my way everywhere I moved; they congratulated me, smiled, shook my hand. I wiped my palm on my suit pants, trying to shove my way past. The bright sunlight stung in my eyes.

At the curb, a uniformed chauffeur opened the back door of a long black car; the bishop climbed in and waved through the window. My father guided me toward the parking lot. I took a last look over my shoulder at the church, but Father Taggart was nowhere to be found.

My confirmation present was a new tennis racket.

*   *   *

On the Sundays after confirmation, I never took communion, but again, neither of my parents seemed to notice I wasn't going to the altar rail. A silent deal had been made: I'd gone through the confirmation ceremony with the others, now I didn't have to bother about church things any longer.

Father Osgood ran the service by himself. Father Taggart was on vacation, my father said. Then in June abbreviated summer services began, which my parents and their friends didn't attend—most of the parishioners didn't go to church during the tennis season. I gradually managed to put Father Taggart out of my mind.

In September, Father Taggart was no longer the assistant minister. My father said he had been transferred to another parish.

Then that winter, Father Taggart's obituary appeared in the local newspaper. His face looked owlish and tired. I clipped it out. This was the first time I'd ever seen a death notice of someone I knew. I wanted badly to cry but my eyes felt dammed.

When I asked my father how the priest had died, he said he knew nothing about the man's passing. It was a terrible shame, but it had happened far away from our town, in another state.

My mother said that she didn't know anything about it, either, but she wouldn't look at me as she spoke. The next time my father went on a business trip and my mother and I were alone for dinner, I asked again how Father Taggart had died.

My mother gripped her glass tight. "He hanged himself," she said, her voice low. "But for God's sakes, don't tell your father I told you."

It was a good thing she was drinking again or she would have noticed the expression on my face as I rushed from the table. In the driveway, I bit my knuckles hard, my teeth digging into the skin until I tasted blood. But I still couldn't cry.

I ran out to the tool shed and sat on the cement floor with a coil of bristly old hemp rope in my lap. I tried to tie it into a noose but didn't know how. The shed was dark and very chilly and smelled of potting soil—the way a grave must smell of dirt. I wound the rope around my neck as tight as I could. It burned the skin of my hands, but I couldn't let go of it. Gagging, I jerked it harder and harder until my palms were raw and my eyes must have been bulging. Finally, finally the tears began streaming down my cheeks. Afterwards, it took me a long time to untangle that rope.

Sometimes I dream that I'm still doing it.

THE FLYING PRINCESS

In Rajasthan, there lived a beautiful princess whose home, between incarnations, was a clay pot. Because her restless spirit had haunted the countryside so shamelessly after her last death, the villagers trapped her in the vessel and buried it on a hillside behind a temple. For years she thrashed against her karma in the round clay prison and wept with loneliness. Finally she lay down and, for a decade, slept.

Then one day a priest dug up her pot to make room for some new ones. He set her down on the edge of a low wall in the temple courtyard. The sun's glare soon heated the clay, and the princess-spirit, whose name was Devi, woke up sizzling.

"Release me!" she commanded.

The priest seemed not to hear her. Rubbing her huge, almond-shaped eyes, she peered out through the clay and past the stone walls of the temple. Everything looked scorched and brown and dry. How would she ever escape this dusty village to find a suitable place for her next birth?

The temple's inner rooms echoed with mournful mantras and the incessant clanging of brass bells. Devi saw throngs of desperate pilgrims climbing over each other to thrust rice balls at the white-robed priests. Dropping the gifts onto braziers, the priests fed the bitter smoke to the monkey-god, Hanuman. His red eyes gleamed out of the altar. When he felt like it, Hanuman flushed a witch from one of the many supplicants who, hoping to be exorcised, had journeyed here by bus, train, and bullock cart from the farthest corners of India.

Devi watched a man with withered legs crawl toward the god on his stomach, cricket-like elbows pumping in the air. Two men carried a woman chained to a board, writhing and shrieking. A boy beat his forehead rhythmically against the floor. Priests shook a woman upside down over the blood-blackened rim of a pit to help her vomit a witch.

Strangest of all these sights, at least to Devi, was that of a tall, light-skinned young man scribbling in a notebook as he talked with a priest. A magnificent green canvas bag hung from his shoulder. He wore cotton trousers and a denim shirt, but despite his Western clothes, Devi could tell he was of royal Indian blood. Yes, he was a young Kashmiri prince from the far north, she was sure—a foreigner to the ways of the Rajasthan desert but eager to learn them, perhaps for his university studies. The stranger had no visible affliction. Yet the brain beneath his thick, black hair seemed to be as agitated as any of the supplicants'. Devi watched his lips moving in his beard:

question! question! question! His eyes crinkled, his mustache squirmed, his teeth clicked.

Suddenly he went silent. A girl collapsed to her knees before him, twitching with palsy. She wore the long brown skirt of a tribal woman. Her hair, tangled and wild, fell over her caved-in cheeks. She searched her open blouse for the buttons she'd clawed off and swallowed, and her little breasts swayed with the motion of her body. Devi could tell that the prince found her beautiful, but the agony in her face made him shudder. He didn't see, as Devi did, the witch that was squatting in the girl's belly with its teeth embedded in her liver.

A crowd pushed the stranger into an adjoining room. He squeezed past hundreds of chanting pilgrims and fled into Devi's courtyard. Immediately a host of witches swarmed up his nose to tickle themselves intimately against his nostril hairs. He sneezed, spraying them across the courtyard. Devi watched him walk toward her clay pot. His face wasn't hard like the face of the sultan who had corrupted and murdered her a century ago. Nor were his eyes blown-out headlamps like the eyes of the hippie boy that, in a later incarnation, she'd frolicked with on the beaches of Goa. No, this man beamed a lonely gaze everywhere; he gathered up pictures and stuffed them into his mind, never finding enough to fill himself.

But Devi had troubles of her own. Her fists pounded the clay pot's wall. How she longed to fly again! Just once before her next birth, she wanted to soar above the treetops. She wanted to drop from the branches onto handsome young men, ride them all night, and leave behind a spell to make them bay in the moonlight whenever they remembered her. Could she still make a man howl?

She watched the stranger sit down on the courtyard wall to question a priest about the pilgrims' beliefs. The priest fed him sugary morsels of karmic enlightenment. The prince swallowed them, his mouth growing sticky. Devi tried to slip a picture of herself into his head, but the place was a jumble of flashing images, like a Bombay cinema house, and if he saw her at all, she was a mere flicker among many.

His questions stopped. He saw the tribal girl again. Thrashing, her lips foaming with spit, she was carried into the courtyard by two burly priests. She tried to bite the men as they pushed her down flat on the ground. A priest set four suitcase-sized slabs of rock along her back. She gasped for breath, her face squashed into the hard dirt. Devi's almond eyes grew damp as she watched. Once she had undergone the same treatment herself, but her spine had snapped before the cure could work.

The pale-skinned stranger couldn't look at the girl. He couldn't *not* look at her. She began to move her lips. Devi saw prayers fluttering around the girl's face, and added some long-forgotten mantras of her own.

"Leave me!" the girl moaned to the witch inside her, feeling it crawl up her throat.

And now Devi sang her prayers in a high, keening voice, tears streaming down her cheeks.

"Out!" The girl's family shouted from the temple doorway. "Out, filthy demon! Carrion-eater! Sister-fucker!"

"*Out!*" the girl shrieked.

And out tumbled the witch from the girl's

mouth—a bearded crone that scuttled away like a cockroach, muttering curses.

"*Aaaah!*" the girl cried.

The sound made the stranger jump to his feet. The canvas bag swung from his shoulder. Clunk! It struck Devi's pot. The princess felt herself tottering, tottering—falling. Sunlight exploded all over her. Shards of pottery lay scattered in the dirt.

Her shell was broken! She could fly again! Expanding to her full size, she rose into the air above the hot, brown earth. Her hair streamed behind her, black and silky. Her golden saree rippled in the wind. She was so graceful, so free!

Her joy lasted only a moment. A careening demon knocked her head over heels into a raucous flock of witches. And now she could see that the air above the temple was as crowded as the rooms inside it. Mantras drifted up from the roof in an enormous net that opened to release thousands of witches into the sky like ashes swirling through clouds of smoke.

Devi watched bald grannies tumble through the air with goats clinging to their withered dugs. Soaring demons gnawed on rotted limbs and sucked the nostrils of skulls. Widows masturbated with their husbands' bones. Old warriors flew by with cats impaled on their swords. A drunken djinn butted Devi to the temple roof, and she rolled off the tiles, groaning. How would she ever escape this fiendish aviary?

As she floated to the ground, she saw priests lifting the heavy stones from the tribal girl's back. The girl sat up, dazed but no longer twitching. Devi let out a sigh of relief. Now the prince knelt beside the girl. What was he doing? He held out a water-bottle. He tilted it over her cupped hands. She raised them to her mouth. Water trickled down her raw throat. And Devi knew that she could trust this man.

The girl staggered into the arms of her waiting family. As the stranger watched her go, Devi slid down the strap of his green shoulder bag and dove inside. The bag had become a nest of stray witches. They cackled and clawed at her golden saree, but she kicked their scaly faces, and they scrambled out, leaving damp putrid trails in the canvas.

Everything was tinted a lovely green, as if she'd found refuge in a cool oasis. "Take me away!" Devi commanded the stranger.

Why was he so slow to move? He stared down the hillside at the village. Sunlight glowed on the mud brick houses. Tinfoil-spangled trucks rested like circus elephants along the street. From inside the bag, Devi could see dark clouds block his landscape, though the air before him was clear. Now all he could see was his own solitude: himself, standing beside the temple, an alien figure looking down at the dusty desert town.

"If you carry me off," she called, "you'll be rewarded!"

But he still didn't hear. How was she going to get this doleful royal donkey to move? Passing her gaze down through his body, she saw his heart pulsing against its prison of ribs, and felt a commotion within her own breast. Humming one of her mantras, she focused all her energy between his legs. Poor albino prunes, they hadn't had a release in a long time. Now the little gonads began to simmer happily.

"Good karma!" Devi cried.

Suddenly he strode away from the temple. She watched an image of the young tribal girl form in his mind. But in his picture, the girl became ageless.

Her eyes grew almond-shaped. Now she was wearing a golden saree instead of a ragged skirt and blouse, and her hair, no longer tangled, fell long and black and silky to her shoulders.

Smiling, Devi curled up against her prince's side and rode back into the world.

COUNTRY GARDENS

On a rare visit to my home town, I go with my father to the shop where he has ordered his tombstone. It looks like any other, except that pressed into the marble above his name is a small bass relief of a World War I biplane.

Strangely, the plane gives me a twinge of longing for something I can't remember from my childhood. I run my fingers over it. Positioned diagonally, it looks ready to wing my father's soul toward Heaven for one final combat mission. I want to lighten the mood by saying this, but decide not to. Though he and my mother took me to church with them for years, I know that he doesn't believe in Heaven any more than I do, and at this point in his life probably wishes he did.

We walk though the town cemetery which is adjacent to the shop. My father is eighty-four, thin and stooped, and he no longer towers above me. "The Mansfields are over here, and there's the Smiths," he says, waving a bony hand toward the graves of his friends, "and here's the Cruickshanks, and the Everetts. . . ." The tombstones seem to lean towards each other, spaced out on the gently sloping lawn among the flower beds and old trees. All the friends, except him, are together still, holding a perpetual lawn party.

For almost fifty years, these same dozen or so couples came to my parents' parties. My mother, having little else to do, planned them for weeks in advance. She hired caterers and butlers, had the hedges trimmed and the grass freshly mowed just before everyone arrived. Afterwards she always complained that the guests bored her to tears.

The late afternoon light flickers in the branches, pours into the cemetery as if beamed through an old bottle, turning the pools of shade a familiar liquid green. The air smells of pine and of the flowers that border the gravel walks. Again I inhale the scents of gin and women's perfume drifting across the lawn beside our house.

"And here's your mother, Jerrett," my father says. He pauses for a moment before a gravestone.

Suddenly the place goes silent. The party has stopped. Where is the clink of glasses, the chatter that the house gave off like a misty glow on those late weekend afternoons? My mother is turned to marble. Never has she been silent at a party, or stationary. And never has my father lingered near her, just looking at her. What can he be thinking of?

There is a blank spot in the grass beside her. Soon he will have to join her there, a marble figure listening to her demands: please, please come home for dinner on time for once, for God's sake stop cutting down trees around the yard before you completely spoil the view from the terrace. He glances slowly from frozen guest to guest. All the couples are standing side by side here. The wives no longer cluster in unobtrusive groups. For eternity, the husbands will have to listen to them, talk to them, and only them. My father hurries away on his long stiff legs, a military pace. I can hardly keep up with him.

At the top of a knoll, we pause to glance back into this glade where all the friends bought their plots years and years ago. A breeze ruffles the tree branches above the guests; leaves swirl around the grass. I see a skirt flick across my peripheral vision; an arm moves, demonstrating a backhand stroke that won a tennis game. The party has begun again behind me.

I could stop it again—turn around and find nothing but a small town graveyard behind me. In a moment I will, once and for all. But first I must be led out onto the terrace to be shown off to the guests.

* * *

Safe for the time being behind the kitchen window, I watched the guests arrive. Their cars were approximately identical—boxy four door sedans, no convertibles, no flashy colors. Men in light summer slacks and sports jackets stepped out of them. The women walked precariously in long dresses and high heeled shoes across the lawn. My parents greeted them on the side terrace. My mother laughed determinedly. My father smiled, holding a man's elbow to steer him toward the bar.

I sipped my tea as slowly as possible. On the table

before me a miniature turtle floated in a glass bowl, its legs and brownish head lying motionlessly in the water. Miss Gilly, my English nanny, had brought me the turtle from her last vacation somewhere in the South. On its back was a painting of a paddlewheel riverboat.

My mother said that the turtle was going to suffocate because of the painting. Miss Gilly promised me, though, that the picture wouldn't hurt the turtle one bit—why else were they called "painted turtles?" I worried about the turtle a lot, and often poked my finger into the water to make sure that it could still move.

Miss Gilly sat at the table beside me in a lumpy old housecoat and slippers, sipping her tea slowly, too, and knitting. Her chins quivered as she moved her lips, counting stitches. The room's heat stuck her dark curls to her forehead. I played with the turtle, lulled by the clicking of her needles, comfortable in the old shirt and dirty dungarees I'd worn to play hide-and-seek with her earlier in the woods. The mud on the knees had dried; I picked it off idly under the table.

Suddenly my mother's voice, giving a sharp order to a butler, came from the hall next door. I pulled my hand from the turtle's bowl quickly. Miss Gilly dropped a stitch.

"You'd better get ready," Miss Gilly said, "Go and change now."

"I haven't finished my tea." I pushed my tongue deep inside the cup to get at the melted sugar at the bottom.

She smiled. "Don't you be a fibber."

"Why do I always have to go meet the guests?"

"Listen, dear, d'you think *I* like going out there

with all those people? I have to stand there until your mother comes and takes you away." She pressed her lips together. "Right, and then I'm supposed to go creeping back to the scullery. Like I was a servant!"

"Aren't you a servant?"

"Certainly not!" Her cheeks went dark pink. "A nanny isn't a servant! When I was in France, my family invited me to meet the guests at their parties. I mingled, I did. I went on trips with them, too."

"Is France where you saw the pyramids?"

"No, that's where I saw the Eiffel Tower. Egypt's where they have the pyramids." She filled her mouth with a canapé and chewed it slowly. "We went out to look at the pyramids in a car with the British ambassador himself. Such a car you've never seen. It had real cut-glass vases in it, with flowers in them."

I stirred the water in the turtle's bowl. "I want to go away to those places."

"I dare say you will one day." She sighed. "But right now you're going to change your clothes."

I picked off another piece of caked mud and gazed out the window, but nothing interesting was there—just the usual gray-haired couples arriving in their gray cars. "What else did you see in Egypt?" I asked, hoping to hear about camels and boat trips on the Nile.

"You're stalling, Jerry."

I took one last glance out the window, then suddenly leaned forward, my forehead touching the glass. "What's *that?*"

A cream-colored whale was swimming up the driveway toward the house. I'd never seen such a car. Its windows were so dark that whoever was inside was hidden. The silver spokes of the wheels blurred like pinwheels. Best of all were the huge bulging, gleaming fins, studded with lights that glowed and tinted the air red.

The car stopped. A man in a uniform walked quickly around the front of the car. He pulled open the back door, gazing straight ahead as if forbidden to actually look upon whoever might emerge.

What happened next was something like the Wizard of Oz: a small plump ordinary-looking man stepped out. He had on a dark suit, not a sports jacket, like the other men, and he was puffing on a cigar. The sun shone off his bald head.

Then a woman emerged from the car in a blur of colors. She wore a silky green dress with a white fur piece over her shoulders. Her hair, which she shook away from her face with a toss of her head, was almost as red as the car's taillights. She put a cigarette in an ivory holder between her lips, and waited.

The man reached up—the woman was taller than him—and produced a flame right out of his fist like a magician. Her head tilted back, and she exhaled a thin steam of smoke. I waited to see what she would do next. Her face broke into a wide red-lipped smile as my father started down the walk toward her.

"Fancy her being here!" Miss Gilly said from behind me.

"Why shouldn't she be?" I asked.

Miss Gilly didn't reply. I saw my mother appear on the walk. She took my father's arm the way the woman with the fur had taken her husband's arm. I'd never seen my mother do that before. Usually she kissed the women guests on the cheek, but she just nodded vaguely at this one. As the woman glided onto the terrace, I pushed my forehead against the glass until Miss Gilly had to yank me back by the collar of my shirt.

"Who are they?" I asked.

"Mr. and Mrs. Miller. The husband used to be a business partner of your father's, years ago, before your parents moved out to the country," she said. "The four of them used to be thick as thieves, the way I heard it."

"Why don't you like her?" I asked.

"Me? I don't even know the woman. It's nothing to do with me, I'm sure." Miss Gilly steered me toward the door, her hand hot on my neck. "Go on upstairs, now. You can bring your turtle with you," she said, "Don't let your mother see you in those filthy trousers. We don't want a row this evening."

Later, frowning in her stiff beige suit, Miss Gilly led me onto the terrace, and, as my mother approached, slipped away. I wore my white pants and blue Sunday school blazer. My combed wet hair dripped under my collar. I stared across the lawn at the woods, wishing I could run off into them.

Marbled clouds fanned across the sky toward a sunset that was singeing the far hillside a dusty purple. The flower beds along the terrace reflected in miniature the brilliant colors overhead, and I heard guests complimenting my mother on the heavenliness of the view. Clusters of them talked about tennis, the Historical Society, crabgrass—just as, my mother always complained, they did at parties week after week, year after year.

But this time someone new was here. Where was Mrs. Miller? I wanted to see her close up. For a moment I caught a glimpse of her white fur, then some women surrounded me, blocking my view. The air went blurry with perfume. Faces dipped down to my level; high-pitched greetings sprayed out of smiles. I pulled my head back as a lady with large nostrils breathed anchovy paste into my face.

Squirming away, I looked around for my father, who sometimes let me stand with the men and listen to tennis stories. But he was too far away, standing taller than the other men on the lawn, ruddy-faced, hawk-nosed, his gray hair looking white in the dimming light. Seeing my mother still coming in my direction, I sidestepped behind a table bristling with canapés.

She circulated among the guests, trailing a clink of ice cubes. The long dress she wore shone dully like a pewter vase. Her frosted hair seemed to need a lot of patting down. As she stopped to talk to people, her eyebrows flew up in exclamation, but her eyes rarely focused on anyone. She looked as if she had what she called a "boring headache." I felt her gaze land on me.

"Where have you *been*, darling?" she asked, suddenly not looking bored any more. She stooped over; faint blue veins were visible in the pale skin of her chest.

I glanced out at the woods one last time. I knew what came next.

Following her, I made my way into the house to the piano in the living room. She waved her hands to make the guests hush. I hammered out "Country Gardens." Usually, the guests ignored my playing after a few minutes, but my mother seemed more determined than usual to get people to listen to me. I glanced up to see her making room for Mrs. Miller near the piano, pointing at me as if to make sure she saw me.

My fingers ran all over the keys like scattering mice. Starting the piece again, I was aware of a white mist that Mrs. Miller's fur made in my peripheral vision. Applause rushed toward me in a wave when the piece was over, then faded into a murmur of voices. My mother, beaming, wandered away to the bar. I bounded down off the piano stool and ran toward the kitchen to eat supper with Miss Gilly.

Afterwards, as I started up the stairs to my room, I felt a hand on my shoulder. Cold bracelets clinked against my neck. My mother was walking unsteadily behind me with a glass in her hand. Her face dipped close to mine. "Just as you always do," she whispered into my face, "exactly the same way. Just pretend we're not even there."

In my attic room, I went to my bed and knelt beside it. Several women were clustered behind my mother in the doorway. They smiled encouragingly at me, holding drinks close to the folds of their dresses as if to hide them. My mother switched on the overhead light. The room grew silent. I clasped my hands on the pillow, my forehead prickling.

"'Our Father, Who art in Heaven. . . . '" My mouth stuck shut.

"That's lovely," my mother whispered, the ice swirling slowly in her glass. "Go on, darling."

"'Hallow-ed be thy name. Thykingdomcome thywillbedone—"

"Jerrett!"

I ground my teeth.

"You're rushing it badly." She sat down hard on the edge of the bed, causing my chin to bounce on my folded hands.

A stain appeared in the sheet, smelling of gin. "You spilled your drink," I said.

"You didn't rush that piece you played on the

piano, darling. I know you can say your prayers just as beautifully." Her fingers gripped my shoulder.

I began more slowly. Dresses rustled behind me. Someone whispered, "Lovely!" Someone sniffled. "Amen," I said, finally finishing. Silence settled over the room like snowflakes in a glass globe. "AND GOD BLESS MISS GILLY!" I screamed, "AND MY TURTLE!"

Someone coughed. I heard a burst of laughter from downstairs.

My mother stood up and groped at the bedpost for support, breathing through her teeth. She squinted down at me. Then she wandered slowly from the room, holding her forehead.

One by one, the women glided out, their dresses whispering on the stairs. In the hallway below, I heard my mother's voice rising. I crawled under the covers and pressed the pillow over my ears. I knew that God was not going to protect Miss Gilly or my turtle, or me, either, for that matter. In fact, if He ever could have protected us, He'd be sure not to now.

The turtle was floating motionlessly in its bowl on the bureau when I got up to put on my pajamas. The picture on its back reflected the overhead light; the paint looked hard and thick. I scraped at it with my fingernail, but the colors seemed to be melted into the shell. I found a sock, dipped it into the water, and picked up the turtle.

Suddenly the door flew open. "What are you doing?" Miss Gilly stood there in her bathrobe, her arms folded across her chest. Her curls were sprung strangely all over her forehead; her face was very red. "Are you trying to wash the painting off that turtle?"

"I have to!"

"It won't come off." She dropped her arms to

her sides. Her shoulders sagged. "Don't you think I tried?"

"You did?"

She nodded.

"I need to fix it," I pleaded. The turtle slipped from my fingers into the bowl with a tiny splash.

"You've fixed things all right—you and your prayers. Your mother's in enough of a state with that woman in the house. Now she's fed up with the lot of us." Miss Gilly glanced down at the turtle, then at me. "Let's see what you've done to the poor little thing."

"I didn't do anything!" My heart began to beat wildly. "Mother says the painting's going to kill him!"

"Nonsense, she doesn't know anything about it." Miss Gilly lay me down on the bed and sat close to me, her hand stroking my cheek.

"Are you sure he's going to be all right?"

Her eyes filled with tears. "I don't know," she said finally.

"You said—" My voice caught in my throat. "You told me the painting wouldn't hurt him."

Her sigh sent a tremor though the mattress beneath me. "It's not *hurting* him, Jerry. He's not in any *pain*." She avoided my stare. "He's very happy here now with you and me," she said, and pointed toward the bowl, where the turtle was paddling, butting its head against the glass. "You see?" She leaned over to hug me.

I didn't look. I held onto her, then let my arms slip from around her neck. My head dropped back onto the pillow like a dead weight.

"Right, then." She tried to smile. "We'll have a nice breakfast in the morning, just the two of us, just like always. Won't we?"

"Okay," I said in a choked voice, knowing better.

She switched off the overhead light and went down the stairs one step at a time, her slippers thumping against the steps.

I closed my eyes. After a while, I dreamed that I lay buried beneath layers of sticky sheets. They tightened around me, hardening. I couldn't move my legs. I couldn't breathe. Crying out, I jerked my head back hard. I was sitting up, awake, gulping in air. The sheet was snarled in a heap at the foot of the bed. My pillow was on the floor.

The room's walls faded into the darkness, contiguous with the night outdoors. Was I really awake? My bedside lamp was still on. My clock said 1:30, later than I'd ever been up. I'd slept for hours. The turtle was still on the bureau. I lifted it out of its bowl, water dripping from my fingers. It looked headless and lifeless in my hand. Finally its head poked out of its shell, and the hard little feet began paddling weakly against my palm. I started breathing again.

Putting on my plaid bathrobe, I dropped the turtle into the pocket for company, and went down the steps. On the second floor landing, I stood very still, rubbing my eyes. Everything looked different, as if the late hour was a new place I was entering.

Voices buzzed from the rooms below the banisters. Treble notes from the piano bounced around like handfuls of ping pong balls on glass. Footsteps clicked across a hardwood floor and vanished into carpet as if over a cliff. To my right, my mother's door was closed. To my left, my father's door was ajar, and a light was on.

I heard someone wandering slowly back and forth—a woman, humming in a faint high voice. I tiptoed up to the door, smelling perfume.

The light was sepia-tinted, as if shining through a basket—the wicker shade of my father's bedside lamp. Mrs. Miller, her back to me, stood over my father's desk. Her shoulders were bare; on the bed lay a heap of dazzling white fur. One of the desk drawers was open. She moved her hand from it; a long cigarette holder rose through the air to her lips, and she drew hard on it, though the cigarette was not lit. Her green dress said "*shhh*" as she turned toward me.

"Hello?" She smiled, and lines fanned out into her cheeks. Her mouth was the color of raspberry sherbet.

I pushed my toes into the soft carpet. "Hello."

"You must be Jerrett," she said, her voice slightly slurred. "I've heard so much about you." Taking a step toward me, she reached out her hand. Her gloved fingers felt as if they were made of velvet. "I'm very pleased to meet you. I'm Mrs. Miller."

"I know," I said.

"You do? Oh, that's good." Her eyes gleamed. She walked past me to shut the door quietly, then sat down on my father's bed beside his desk. "You know, I came upstairs to find you," she said, wrapping the white fur over her shoulders. "He said your room was upstairs, so I looked into all of them. Then once I was in here . . . I got distracted."

"My room's in the attic."

"I *see*." She glanced up at the ceiling. "Is it nice up there?"

"It's too quiet."

"I'll bet it is," she said. "Would you . . . like to sit down?" She patted my father's desk chair. Her hand moved up and down gaily, as if her palm were resting on an invisible spring. The movement made me smile, and this made her laugh, her eyes widening.

I could see that she was drunk. I knew that my mother got drunk sometimes, but she did it quietly, ashamedly, as if her gin was a medicine she had to drink to keep her headaches away. Mrs. Miller seemed to do it just to make people laugh for no reason. I climbed onto the chair and sat down.

She sat on the edge of the bed, her legs crossed, smiling at me. Her hair glowed red in the lamplight; seeing it brush against her neck made my own skin feel faintly warm. It was rude to stare at her, I knew, but at this late hour, all the rules were different.

"I heard that some ladies got to hear you say your prayers," she said finally. "I'd have loved to have heard that."

"I hated it." I squeezed the knot of my bathrobe cord.

"Yes, I suppose it couldn't have been much fun, performing for an audience," she said. "I'm not the slightest bit religious. But when I wasn't invited to your prayers, an awful sorrow, a rage almost . . . went stabbing through me."

"Why?" I asked.

She gazed past me and drew on her cigarette holder. "I felt like the woman in the fairy tale who wasn't invited to the child's christening," she said. "There was a sewing machine or something in the story, do you know the one I mean?"

I nodded. "I think she put a spell on the house."

"Ah!" Mrs. Miller raised one hand in front of her face and slowly wiggled her gloved fingers in the direction of the doorway. I laughed, squirming in my chair. "But anyway, I thought, I'll just go upstairs and see Jerrett by myself. I probably won't ever . . . get another chance." She blinked several times. "Oh, you do look like your father. I'm so glad you came to see me."

"I heard you in here. I was curious."

"I like curious people. Brave people." She smoothed the fur against her neck. "Tell me about yourself. Do you get lonely living in the attic?"

My mouth fell open.

"If I had a wonderful little boy like you, I surely wouldn't keep him in. . . ." Her voice faded out.

"Don't you have any children?" I asked finally.

She pushed out her lower lip and tilted her head sideways.

"Maybe you will," I said.

"That's sweet." Her hand lighted on my wrist.

I didn't move. The walls glowed with the pattern of the woven lampshade. I'd never been in this room in my life; it was no longer part of the house. The noise from the party was far below us; we were floating above it in a big basket suspended from a balloon.

She turned and picked something up from the desk. I noticed again the open drawer.

"What were you looking for?" I asked her.

"I don't know . . . anything. I just enjoyed walking around. It's been twenty-four years since I've been invited. . . ." Her lips dived down at the corners. "Anyway, I've always wanted to see the house he'd gotten out here, and his room and—and you. . . ."

I leaned forward to peer into her hand. She was holding a tiny model of a World War I biplane. Its usual place was among some ledgers and rubber stamps in the back of the drawer. I'd found it there once while exploring the room, and sometimes I liked to take it out to play with. The propeller had long ago broken off. The cloth on the wings had disintegrated, leaving just the wire skeleton.

"You have to be careful with that," I said. "It's old."

"Old." She nodded slowly. "I'll put it back. I just wanted to hold it." When she set it on the desk, she had to push her other hand down against the bedspread to keep from tilting over, as if the plane had been giving her ballast.

"My father was a pilot once," I said. "I think his plane looked like that one."

"He used to talk about it—such exciting stories. I'll bet he's told you some, hasn't he?"

"No." I stood up to have another look at the plane.

Her forehead rippled with lines. "He doesn't talk much any more, does he?"

I shook my head, pushing the plane across the desk top. I left it there and sat down on the edge of the bed. The carpet was fuzzy under my bare toes. Suddenly I felt something move against my thigh. It startled me so much that I almost slapped at it. Then I remembered my turtle and reached into my bathrobe pocket.

Her eyes followed my every movement. "What's the matter?"

"It's just my turtle." I rested it on the palm of my hand so that the light shone on it. It's head went back into its shell.

"Oh, can I see?"

I reached out my hand and she picked up the turtle with her thumb and forefinger. "Hello, there," she said, "Oh, he's got a pretty picture on his back."

"I wish he didn't."

"Why?"

"The picture's going to kill him."

"Your mother said that, didn't she?"

"How did you know?"

She dropped her eyes. "I used to have turtles like these when I was a girl. Grownups used to give them to me. They always . . . died, I'm afraid. But the truth is, Jerrett. . . ." She leaned forward and gazed at me. "It had nothing at all to do with the paintings on them."

"It didn't?" I sat up straight in my chair.

She shook her head slowly. "The ones without paintings were no different from the others."

"How come?"

"Well, I think. . . ." She raised her hand slowly until the turtle was inches from her mouth. "I think they're just not made to live in captivity. It's their nature."

"Oh," I said. "I never knew that."

She nodded, pursing her lips. Slowly the turtle's head stretched out toward them.

"He hardly ever comes out if somebody's holding him," I said.

"Maybe he knows he's among friends."

She set the turtle down on the bedspread, and we watched it walk around, exploring. The room was warm and smelled sweet from her perfume. I heard the piano tinkling faintly, off-key, far below us. The balloon basket we were in swayed high above the house.

Mrs. Miller's fingers pushed down the bed, creating a hill for the turtle to crawl down. I noticed that the skin around her knuckles was wrinkled and her glossy fingernails were bitten down. Suddenly the hand was gone. The bed rose fast, and the turtle flipped over onto its back, its legs paddling in the air.

"Oh, no!" Mrs. Miller was staring at the door.

Slow, tired footsteps approached along the landing outside. I grabbed the turtle and slipped it into my bathrobe pocket. She clutched the fur against her chest.

I heard a squeaking sound—a hand sliding along the banister railing. My mother, leaning on the railing as she walked, made that sound sometimes. I recognized her footsteps. They clicked onto the hardwood floor in front of her room, paused while she must have opened the door, then vanished onto her carpet inside. Her door slammed with a crack that jiggled the wicker lampshade.

Mrs. Miller let out all her breath. The lines around her eyes deepened. "The party seems to be over," she said.

"That's too bad."

"I think so, too." She leaned forward, her face level with mine. "Are you going to tell anyone I was here?" she asked. Her white fur seemed to tremble against her throat.

I shook my head.

She held my chin lightly in her hand. Her lips were cool and wet against the corner of my mouth. "It'll be our secret."

I smiled. "All right."

Grabbing the fur as it was about to slip off her, she lurched out of the room.

Early the next morning when I walked outdoors, dew was glistening in the rows of tire-tracks on the grass. I found the ones where the huge car had been resting; they were deeper than the others. My father's car backed out of the garage; I caught a glimpse of his white tennis hat in the window as he drove past.

The terrace was strewn with cocktail napkins. Hot sunlight soaked up the morning dampness, igniting the yellow forsythia bushes, bleaching the sky light blue. Already the day was too bright.

My turtle moved in the pocket of my shirt. Holding my hand gently over it, I rushed down the lawn and into the woods. Now the glare was gone; the air was cool. I hardly noticed the branches brushing against me as I ran.

Arriving at the brook, I sat on the bank. Slowly I set the turtle down. It's feet made tiny tracks in the sand, and I felt a surge of loneliness rush through me, making me squeeze my eyes shut for a long moment. Finally, I gave the turtle a nudge, and it paddled off into the water. I watched it swim toward a bend where the brook would widen out and carry it far away.

* * *

I turn back toward the glade where the marble party guests stand leaning toward each other on the grass. The sun has gone down, leaving a chill in the air. Clouds have congealed in the sky above the graveyard. All the variations of green on the lawn have turned the same shade of gray. Even the flowers along the paths seem to have been etched, albeit elegantly, in black and white. A narrow pond beside the glade reflects the sky, its water motionless as ice.

Mrs. Miller has not been invited to this party, but she is here anyway, a flicker of red between two distant trees. She stands on the grass in front of a pale, whale-shaped mausoleum, humming faintly to herself. —Hello! she cries gaily, seeing me at the top of the hill, and throws me a kiss from long gloved fingers. A hand reaches up to light her cigarette for her. Smiling, she draws on it through the ivory holder; plumes of smoke envelop her like white fur, and she vanishes into them.

I search among the trees for a squat figure in a beige suit. Where is Miss Gilly now? I remember that when we played hide and seek in the woods, just as I'd start to get panicky because I couldn't find her, she'd call out to me. —Yoo hoo! I'd turn toward the voice, and there she'd be, standing beside a tree as if she'd been there all along. I'm certain she would call out to me now, if only she could.

Of the three women I remember from that party, only one is left here. I ought to go back and visit my mother's grave. The few times I've come to see it, I've been with my father, and I've been too aware of him standing at attention beside me to remember her clearly.

I could tell him I want to stay with her a few minutes by myself. He'd gladly wait in the car. He's straining toward it already, gazing diagonally up the hill now as if aiming toward distant clouds.

I stop walking. Just for a moment I want to remember the late afternoon sun sparkling on the grass; I want to feel the warmth rising from the lawn into the perfumed air. I want to hear the murmur of voices again and the off-key notes of a far-away piano.

But the party here grinds on in silence like teeth in sleep. The tombstones echo my mother's pewter-colored dress, her frosted hair, the ice gone motionless in her glass. Her face reflects the gathering darkness. Leaning toward the empty space in the grass beside her, she raises her head slowly and squints up the hill at me.

I hurry away with my father; I'm his accomplice, finally. I'm sorry, but I don't want to go down that hill again. I do not want to face my mother alone.

She might ask me —for God's sake, Jerrett, why have you left me here? Why have you left me with these people who bore me so?

PEBBLES

My grandfather, a pauper at the end and a lifelong atheist, spent the last months of his life building a church on the grounds of a state mental hospital, where he lived in the old folks' wing. All day he collected pebbles and pressed them down in long straight lines on a dirt area that the staff called the recreation yard. Sometimes he knelt down under one of the oak trees and called on the Lord to reveal exactly where He wanted the walls erected.

My grandfather was a huge man with a smile that collapsed his toothless mouth and made you think of a jack-o-lantern left outdoors too long after Halloween. But it was still a salesman's smile: sometimes he could be heard discussing the price of stained glass to Jesus in the same hearty voice he'd used to pitch vegetable peelers, home wine-making kits, and all the other products that had so often landed him in bankruptcy courts.

His behavior was no stranger than that of many other patients, such as the lady who sang obscene nursery rhymes all day, or the man who collected his drool in a jar, or another man who carried a cardboard sword and called himself Robert E. Lee. People got used to seeing my grandfather lurching about the grounds in his baggy raincoat and squashed fedora hat, searching for small stones. At first no one paid much attention to his church. But after a while, it gave him so much to talk about at meals that everyone began discussing it, as if they, too, could see walls rising outside the dining room window.

One Sunday morning, the old man announced that the church was finished. He cleaned himself up for the first time since he'd arrived at the hospital. He brushed his white hair, shaved the stubble from his chin, put on his double breasted suit and a wide hand-painted tie. Then he walked out onto the yard and, standing at one end of his pebbly diagram, delivered a sermon. No one came to hear it, but several residents sat in canvas chairs under a nearby tree to watch him wave his arms and shout across the grounds. After the service, he made a sharp right-angle turn around an invisible altar and left by a gap in the pebbles. He rejoined the others under the tree, mopping his brow with a big checked handkerchief.

The next Sunday, five or six residents got dressed up and attended his service. The following week, there were a dozen or more. Ladies took dresses they hadn't worn in thirty years out of suitcases. Men brushed out suits and made special trips to the thrift shop in town to select colorful neckties. The staff helped them drag chairs out to the pew area, and some staff brought chairs for themselves as well.

Soon, nearly everyone was attending the Sunday services. A choir was formed, which the old man rehearsed and directed. Someone supplied a wooden cross. The staff made an altar out of orange crates and a table cloth. Robert E. Lee left his sword outside, the drooling man put his jar on the altar as an offering, and the woman with the obscene nursery rhymes recited them only to herself during the services, her voice getting quieter each week until finally her lips stopped moving altogether.

As long as the weather stayed warm, it was pleasant to sit in the sunlight surrounded by lines of pebbles, listening to the old man's voice fading in and out of consciousness. When he pointed at the Bible scenes he said were depicted in the stained glass windows, everyone gazed up, seeing not merely expanses of blue summer air, but New Testament pictures in blazing red and gold. The preacher's sermons were quite lucid and full of good jokes. One Sunday, he married two of the residents. The staff began to bring their families for services. The local newspaper featured him on its church news page.

He died in the fall, just as the weather was growing chilly. On a gray Sunday morning, the residents and staff put on warm clothes and held a memorial service for him in his church. Then all the pebbles were raked up before the rains could wash them away. The residents selected bright colored ones to keep in their rooms. There were enough left over to border a flower garden, which was named after him and dedicated with a bronze plaque.

The church was the only successful venture of my grandfather's life.

THE TURQUOISE BALLOON

Miss Gilly, my English nanny, kept her mail in a big square biscuit tin with the royal family's portrait on the lid. Her favorite family member was Princess Elizabeth, who she said reminded her of the British Ambassador's child she'd taken care of years before in Paris. When she received letters from her friends she always read them to me. But one year just before the Christmas when I was nine, a letter arrived addressed to "Miss Alma Gilly" that she wouldn't read aloud. She tried to interest me in its stamps with palm trees on them.

"Who's the letter from?" I asked. "Who?"

Her cheeks flushed red. "It's from a man I once knew. He's coming to New York and he wants to see me—it's preposterous!"

A stack of similar envelopes lay on her bureau beside the open cookie tin. I counted twenty of them, each with a seal on the back which she said was from the British Embassy in some South American country. I demanded an explanation.

Holding her lumpy old bathrobe together at her chest, she sat down on the bed. "Once upon a time," she said, "I met a foreign service gentleman in Paris. He wanted to be my friend. We went for walks in the parks." She squeezed her hands together in her lap. "He took me up for a balloon ride, and asked me to marry him."

I'd often been intrigued by a faded photograph she kept in her tin of an enormous hot-air balloon. I stared at the figures in the basket below the balloon. The woman, wearing a long old-fashioned dress, had Miss Gilly's bulging eyes and plump cheeks, but the curls that fringed her head were light instead of dark gray. I didn't recognize the giddy smile on her face at all. The man beside her stood stiffly in a white suit and jaunty straw boater. I made out a neat mustache. She took a long look at the photo before taking it from my hand.

"That was twenty years ago, and he writes to me every year. He says he still wants to marry me." She rolled her eyes. "He's invited me to have dinner with him at the Waldorf Astoria Hotel in New York."

I sat down on the bed beside her. "Are you going to marry him?"

"Of course not—don't be silly!" She pursed her lips. "He must be an old man by now. Sixty-four years old. And I'm nearly fifty."

"Then why do you want to have dinner with him?"

Miss Gilly wiped her forehead. "I don't know."

I bounced on the bed, begging to hear about Paris, the balloon, her friend. She put the letters back into the tin and put it on the top shelf of her closet, out of my reach.

Since she wouldn't tell me anything more about the foreign service gentleman, I've had to make him up.

* * *

As he walks with her through the park beside the Seine, she smiles at the children sailing boats in the fountain pools. Can she ever appreciate a mature love, he wonders, and not just the dependent adoration of a child? For once, her employers' little girl is not chaperoning them. Yet he's the one who feels nervous. He has just been assigned a new posting, and today is his last chance to propose to her. He's beginning to think he'll never find the right words unless something extraordinary happens. If only he had time to write them to her. . . . He pauses to stare at a statue of a woman on a pedestal.

"Ridiculous," Alma says. "A person standing up there half-naked in public." She says she prefers statues like Lord Nelson in Trafalgar Square that make you feel proud of your country.

"Quite," he says.

Feeling hot in his too-tight suit, he undoes as many of his waistcoat buttons as he dares and takes deep breaths of the river-scented air. A lone frog croaks somewhere. He gazes at a man and wife fishing from their houseboat, and feels about to explode with longing. The husband is robust, red-faced; the Englishman is aware of himself as pale and chinless, a lonely, middle-aged civil servant—

"Oh, a fête!" she says, as children run squealing past them. Ahead are gaily striped tents; hurdy-gurdy music and the scent of candied almonds float through the air. "And just look at that—"

He's seen it, too. An enormous turquoise-colored balloon sways gently in the breeze. It seems to be gazing up at the clouds as it strains against the net that tethers it. Suddenly he knows that this is his chance. He has never held her hand before, but now he grabs it and rushes toward the balloon.

"Wait!" she cries. "What if its ropes break?"

She's staring wide-eyed at this great circus-colored airship. She hasn't shaken off his hand; she's squeezing it, in fact! He thrusts a handful of franc notes at the man beside the basket and pulls Alma with him. The little wicker gate opens. They stumble through. A photographer with a big box camera steps up.

Alma grips his arm with both hands, smiling giddily at the camera. The flash powder explodes, obliterating the children, the tents, the park. Incandescence echoes in the air. By the time they have rubbed it from their eyes, the treetops are slowly sinking beneath them. They rise slowly. Watching her gaze down, her soft curls fluttering in the breeze, he forgets the churning of his stomach. Never has he felt so light before, so bold. The Eiffel Tower shimmers in the sunlight. Traffic sounds fade; all he hears is the faint harp song of the balloon's cords.

"The river's so blue—just like a silk ribbon," Alma says. "When I was small, I always fancied a ribbon like that for my hair."

He stares at her face, trying to untangle calm, persuasive sentences in his mind. Rooftops spread out below. His necktie, loose from his waistcoat, flaps like a kite-tail in the warm breeze. Alma is still holding onto his arm as if he is what is keeping her buoyant. Now! he thinks— But suddenly the basket jerks; he feels its floor drop beneath him. He staggers, the blood rushing from his face. The balloon sways, suspended in space as if its ropes have broken loose from the earth. "Alma—" he gasps, and lurches toward her. "Stay with me! Marry me!" Blindly he kisses her eyes, her cheeks. Never has he done anything like this before. "Please, please stay with me!" He presses against her, a moan flying out of his throat.

She shakes her head hard. "What are you *doing*?"

He drops to his knees. His hat tumbles off and rolls between her shoes. Half rising, he wraps his arms around her waist, buries his face against her breast.

She stops straining backwards. "There, there," she murmurs, and cradles his head. Gently she tucks his necktie into his waistcoat. "How could I ever leave the child?" she says. "I don't know, I can't think—" She touches the place on her cheek where he kissed her.

He hears the laughter of children in the park below. The rooftops come closer, the treetops expand, the ground tilts strangely. His heart is a frog kicking as it falls through space. He stumbles upright, groping for his hat. "I'm terribly sorry," he says. The dampness in his eyes blurs her face. "I've ruined it all."

Biting her lip, she takes one more look over the side of the basket. "Oh, no . . ."

"I'll write to you, Alma—"

They leave the park in silence. The tremor in his legs lasts all the way to her embassy residence. She stands beside its gate, waiting. "It was the loveliest sight I ever saw," she says.

He opens his mouth, but no sound comes out. He shakes her hand.

Then he watches her walk slowly away from him and disappear through the heavy door. For a moment, she stands at the window. Then she is gone, and the world is a sunless, empty place. He drifts off into the rest of his life, into the silence of years. Already he is beginning to fill it with the words of the first of his letters to her.

* * *

This was the plan: Miss Gilly was to take me to New York for a day's sightseeing and drop me off at my father's office, where a Christmas party would be in progress. My father would take me home on the train while she went to have dinner with the English man.

"I don't want to go to the office," I said, glaring at Miss Gilly in the elevator. I didn't like the idea of the place: my father's company manufactured ladies' lingerie, a source of embarrassment when this had somehow gotten out at school. And I didn't care at all for the way Miss Gilly inspected herself in the elevator's mirrored panel, either. She never worried about how she looked at home.

"Wild woman of Borneo!" she said, trying to push down her springy gray curls. "I can't walk into a grand hotel looking like this!"

"That's true," I said.

She turned sideways, pulling open her second-hand fur coat, which was speckled with snowflakes. "I just wish I wasn't so bloody fat!"

"Weren't you fat, before?"

She smoothed her suit jacket down over her bosom and straightened the silk scarf at her throat. "Oh, I was always plump. He never seemed to mind. I reckon he figured if I was a beauty, I wouldn't want anything to do with a timid old bachelor like him." She laughed. "But in point of fact, Jerry, he's made something of himself. He's the attaché to the British ambassador to Brazil now."

"So?"

"So he can afford to give me a nice night out. I deserve to be treated like a lady once in a while."

"I know where Brazil is." It was a stop on a Pirate and Traveler board game we often played. If you landed on Brazil, you had to stay there for four rolls of the dice, which seemed forever to me. But not to Miss Gilly. She always said it seemed like a lovely place to rest. "It's where they have the vampire bats," I said, scowling.

Miss Gilly knelt beside me, her brow furrowing. "You're worried about being left with your father in that office, aren't you? I suppose I shouldn't just leave you there."

"He always has to stay at work late."

"We'll see, dear. I'm sure you'll like the Christmas party."

At the one at church last winter, I'd had to make *papier maché* sheep for a creche. "I'm too old for Christmas parties," I told her.

When the elevator door slid open, I was sure we were on the wrong floor. Before me stood a nearly naked woman. It wasn't a real woman, of course, just a very life-like mannequin wearing a Christmas bow over her belly button and a lacy white bra and panties manufactured by the company. She was holding out her hand out toward me. In her palm was a big glass marble, blue-green tinted, clear as a crystal ball. Dozens, perhaps hundreds of these gleaming marbles filled a pool around the pedestal she was standing on. I approached her slowly, transfixed. "You come away from there this instant!" Miss Gilly grabbed my arm, her face flushed.

"S'all right," someone said. A bald man in a dark suit ambled up to us, sloshing a paper cup. "He can have a marble."

Miss Gilly stepped back, her fur coat bristling. "Who do you think *you* are?"

"I think I am—" The man bowed at his waist. "Edgar Bernbaum, Assistant Vice President, Marketing. At your service, madame."

"Mr. Bird-bom, I'll thank you to show us to Mr. Langley's office. This boy is his son—"

"No kidding?" The man blinked at me. His beaky nose did make him look like a bird—a bald, bespectacled parrot in a gray suit. "Well, then, he gets all the marbles he wants. Help yourself, buddy."

Ignoring Miss Gilly, I took the marble from the woman's hand and dropped it into my overcoat pocket. The woman's glossy lips seemed to smile at me. I stared at the mannequin over my shoulder as Miss Gilly yanked me down a corridor after Mr. Bernbaum.

The office was a maze of passages whose frosted glass partitions were only as high as the top of my head. Through doorways I caught glimpses of cubicles where bowls of punch were laid out on desks. People were singing "God Rest Ye Merry Gentlemen" in off-key voices.

"Straighten your tie!" Miss Gilly whispered at me as Mr. Bernbaum opened a door ahead of us and then backed away as if awed by something inside the room. I walked in; the door shut, the music vanished.

"Well, hello there, Jerrett." My father stood up

from behind an enormous desk and reached across it.

"Hello," I said, leaning forward to shake his hand. I could feel his eyes inspecting my tie, blazer, and slacks. His office was the size of our dining room at home, with oil paintings on the wall and a huge window behind his desk. I gazed out at tall buildings that rose like blocks of black granite through swirling snowflakes.

"How do you like this place, young man?" My father's bushy brows formed sideways question marks.

"I don't know," I said, feeling sweaty.

Folding his hands on his desk, he asked me what sights I'd been seeing. I wanted to tell him about Mr. Bernbaum's offer, but he looked too important, in his dark suit and gray silk tie, to be interested in marbles. Miss Gilly said she wanted to go "do something with her hair." I gave her a panicky look, but she left anyway. An awkward silence followed. Someone knocked on the door.

A young woman rushed though the door on a gust of perfume. "Laura's on the line for you, sir," she said to my father.

"Jerrett—" My father stood up, pointing with his chin toward the door. At home he sometimes excused me from the room in the same way after picking up the telephone. I stepped into the hall, letting out my breath. The door clicked shut.

I looked for Miss Gilly up one corridor and down the other, my fists clenched at my sides, but she was nowhere to be seen. Gradually my panic faded. I decided to look for the woman with the marbles. In the first office I came to, somebody had hung out a lady's stretched nylon stocking with gaily wrapped presents in it. On a desk some bottles surrounded a bowl of purple punch; steam rose from a miniature iceberg floating in it. I ladled myself a big paper cup full. It tasted fizzy and left a glow in my stomach. When I walked away from the table, the floor tilted strangely beneath my feet.

I was lost. Walls of glass kept rising up before me. Fluorescent lights overhead made the air vibrate around my face. I reached into my pocket to feel the marble, as if it would orient me, but I'd left it in my overcoat in my father's office.

The maze of corridors led on and on. In one cubical some men and women were dancing. As I walked in, smiles froze and laughter stopped. At first I enjoyed producing silence wherever I looked, but soon I got exasperated, and ducked only into offices that seemed empty. I was helping myself to more punch in one when a man stepped up beside me.

"Ah, young Master Langley," he said, tipping an imaginary hat. His horn-rimmed glasses tilted on his nose. "Mr. Bird-balm, at your service. Have you found the nymph of the marbles yet?"

I shook my head, grinning.

"She's a dream, isn't she? And all those marbles—like finding a pirate's chest full of jewels." He squatted down beside me, his lips bending into a smile. "D'you still call them clearies?"

I nodded. "That's right."

"And do kids still walk around holding them in front of their eyes?" He squinted through a circle he made with his thumb and index finger. "And everything looks like it's under water?"

"Yes," I said. "Do you know where she is?"

"Where indeed?" He sighed. "Through the enchanted forest. At the end of the rainbow."

I cocked my head. "What did you say?

"First right at the end of the hall, just past Accounting," he said, standing unsteadily. "*Bon voyage!*"

I got lost again; all I found were more corridors, more cubicles, but no pool of marbles with a woman standing in it. I stopped for a drink at each unattended punch bowl I came to until I began to feel very queasy. When I came upon a darkened office that seemed empty, I ducked inside, looking for a place to sit down.

I stopped, bubbles rising in my throat. Someone moved. A man and a woman were on a couch, the woman sitting on the man's lap. Her white bra glowed in her open blouse. The man's hand rose toward it. Suddenly she struggled to her feet. The man stood too, trying to embrace her.

I heard loud footsteps behind me. "*Just what d'you think you're doing?*" Miss Gilly's voice knocked the man off balance.

The woman fumbled with her blouse. I lurched forward without meaning to, but Miss Gilly grabbed me by the collar, my shirt tightening against my throat. A loud burp jumped out of my mouth, echoing in the cubical like a frog in a well. Then she let go and I had to grab the door frame to stay on my feet. The man and woman had vanished. My stomach was churning.

"Where on earth have you been?" Miss Gilly asked.

"Was looking for you," I mumbled.

"The goings-on in this place!" she muttered. As she tried to straighten my necktie, she must have caught a whiff of my breath, and began scrubbing my face with her handkerchief. I squirmed away.

"Stay *still*, you little heathen! You're going to upset everything!"

I escaped to the bathroom across the hall. The tiles shimmered light blue. The whole place was blurry, as if under water. I managed to wash my face and focus on the mirror. I was strangely glassy-eyed. In the corridor, Miss Gilly pushed a peppermint into my mouth. The sweet taste made something start to rise in my stomach like a big bubble through sludge. Open doorways flickered by in pale waves.

In his office, my father had his topcoat on. "Sorry I didn't have time to show you around, son" he said. "But I've got to leave now."

Miss Gilly stared at him. "Aren't you going to take him home?"

"Me?"

"I thought that was the *plan*, Mr. Langley." There was a strange catch in her voice. "I was going to go on to dinner with my friend."

My father touched his forehead. "I must have forgotten."

I only half-heard this—I was remembering the marble I'd left in my topcoat, and began moving blurrily around the desk toward it.

"I've got an appointment, so I'm going to have to take a later train home," he said. "But I could drop him off at the station."

"What, and have him ride that train all by himself?"

"He seems perfectly capable." My father glanced down at me.

Miss Gilly frowned. "I'm not so sure."

I needed badly to get hold of the marble. I yanked the coat toward me from the chair, but the chair yanked back. Then I was off balance and the marble was bouncing on the hardwood floor at my feet. I sank to my knees, the sudden movement making me seasick.

"Are you all right?" Miss Gilly asked.

My mouth formed the word "no," but suddenly a different sound burst out of my throat, along with a long gushing spasm of purple liquid. More followed, churning up out of my stomach. I pitched forward, sprawling face-first into a sticky warm puddle.

"Oh, Jerry, what have you *done?*" Miss Gilly's voice was higher than I'd ever heard before. She knelt beside me. Sitting up, I could see clearly again. I noticed for the first time that she had on make-up. Her cheeks were round and smooth; her curls lay in a soft fringe around her forehead.

"What the hell's going on here?" My father's shoes moved away from the puddle.

"I think he's got into the punch, Mr. Langley." Miss Gilly's lower lip began to quiver.

"Why weren't you looking after him?"

"I—I don't know what I could have been thinking of."

I leaned forward, my necktie dripping. "The marble," I croaked.

"Well, never mind." My father moved toward his desk. "I'll get him to the train somehow."

The office was terribly quiet. I didn't dare look at Miss Gilly.

Her hand fell slowly, and she began to stroke the hair from my forehead. "It's all right, dear," she said, "I'll stay with you."

* * *

I remember riding in silence on the train back to Connecticut. I sat hunched over, squeezing the marble I'd somehow managed to rescue from my father's office. A chilly wind blew through the car. My mouth tasted rancid and I knew I stank. I was sure Miss Gilly could smell me. Pressing one hand against her cheek, she stared past me out the window. Her curls were flat and damp on her forehead.

I picture the marble lying like a crystal ball in my hand. When I look at it from one side, I see Miss Gilly facing the window, her soggy fur coat gathered around her. From another angle, I see a rounded reflection of the city she is staring at. It glides past the train, building after building falling into the night without a sound.

Far across the city she sees a man in a white suit and a neat mustache sitting in a hotel dining room. A candle flickers on his table. Beside his linen napkin a small package waits. It is tied with a blue silk ribbon and wrapped in silvery paper that matches his hair. He imagines her unwrapping the package. Inside is a velvet-lined box that he will open for her. He can picture her face when she sees the ring—the face of a young woman gazing down from the sky at a city sparkling before her on a bright, sunny morning. He takes her hand in his, feeling the softness, the plumpness, the warmth. His breath stops as he slides the ring onto her finger.

He waits and waits for her. His gaze moves many times from the package to the door. The dining room is empty now. The candle has burned down to a wax stump. He tucks his necktie tighter into his waistcoat and takes a long look at his watch. Now he can no longer imagine slipping the ring onto her finger, or picture the way her face might look. He hears the box click shut. The silvery paper wraps itself slowly around it. The ribbon loops over and under the package. Its ends twist into a bow. The box falls from his hand into his jacket pocket. He stands and moves slowly toward the dining room door. He walks out into the last years of his life, through the vampire-infested jungles of Brazil, to the white granite embassy rising on a cliff above a sea where the ships of pirates and travelers float motionless, never docking.

"I'm sorry," I finally managed to say. I stared up at her.

She blinked. The train bumped along the elevated track. Snowflakes slanted down out of the darkness, dripped sideways across the window.

"It's probably all for the best," she said quietly.

I tried to give her the marble, but she wouldn't take it.

WHITE HIGHLANDS

Heinrich Louw was the last Afrikaaner farmer in the White Highlands of Kenya. The old man would never have sold his land if his daughter had not tricked him into signing the papers. For weeks, he stumbled about the house in a rage; she had to dump the contents of his drawers into suitcases while he slept. He would not listen to her talk of going "home" to South Africa. This is my land, he shouted at her; I will not move from it!

Louw had come to Kenya from the south forty-six years before, but his method of running a farm had not changed. Laborers he considered lazy were beaten. If one of them was careless and broke a piece of machinery, goats or chickens were confiscated from him as compensation. Louw did not approve of spoiling the natives by starting a school on his property, as some of his British neighbors had done. As a white man, however, he recognized his duty to impart the teaching of civilization to the heathen races. Every Sunday at seven o'clock he stood on the front step of his farmhouse and shouted from the Bible at his laborers. The men and their families huddled on the ground beneath a big gum tree, shivering in the early morning mist. Louw knew as little of the local African dialects as he did of English, but he was confident that the depth and volume of his voice, combined with the sight of his long gray beard rising and falling on his barrel chest, gave his message the proper authority.

His words were also backed by the authority of Time: a massive bronze alarm clock stood on the step beside him as he preached. Laborers who arrived late for the service received less than their usual weekly rations of flour and salt. Those who knew what it was grew to hate the clock as much as they did the sight of its master.

Louw's Afrikaaner neighbors were suspicious of him, for he did not worship with them; in fact, they rarely saw him. His only appearance at the small Dutch Reformed church near the town occurred when he attended the funeral of his wife. She had borne him but one child late in life, a daughter he named Johanna. He determined to teach the girl all he knew about the land. In his later years, it was Johanna who kept the farm going, tramping about the fields and barns, supervising the plantings and harvests, keeping the accounts and making the decisions that less and less frequently required consultation with her father. And it was Johanna who finally, in her fortieth year, had the papers drawn up that would deed the farm to an African cooperative society. By this time, the old man could not see well, and would sign anything she put before him.

But Louw refused to leave. His daughter explained to him over and over that Kenya was now an independent nation: Did he want to live in a country ruled by heathens? If she hadn't sold the farm, she was sure that the new government would have confiscated it. All the other Afrikaaners in the Highlands had already left. Their time was up here.

Exasperated, she spoke of the old rumor the neighbors had told about him: that he had fled South Africa to avoid being tried for the death by suffocation of a Zulu boy he had caught stealing, had locked in a trunk, and then forgotten about. Was that why he would not leave? The old man scratched his white beard. It was too long ago to remember, he said. This was his land, here. He would not abandon it.

He went to sit on the front step of the house among the boxes and barrels, the rusted plowshares and broken wagon parts. He listened to the cries of the African children playing near the gum tree, he watched the sun burn down through the branches and turn the fields dark red. He had claimed this land from darkness and caused it to bring forth crops, and he saw that it was good.

On the day that they were to leave, Johanna argued with him all morning and all afternoon, while the servants packed the van with crates and suitcases. But when everything was ready, he still would not move from the front step. His daughter stood before him, her feet planted apart, her arms folded. Louw gripped the wooden railing with both hands. His long white beard glowed with the last rays of the sun. Johanna removed her spectacles to clean them on the hem of her dress, and for the moment that her eyes were bare they shone dark and sharp with fear. But when she straightened her back and replaced her spectacles, her voice was calm. She shouted for the servants.

Usually they padded sullenly about after her commands, but today they came running, grins breaking out on their faces, as if they had been waiting for this particular command for many years.

Though Louw was past eighty, he was not frail. It took Johanna and the two Africans nearly an hour to get him bound and secured in the van. He could not be contained in the front seat, for he battered his head against the door until it flew open and he tumbled out onto the dirt. The African children who had gathered to watch scrambled to safer positions behind the gum tree. Finally the old man was wedged securely into a narrow space between crates in the back of the van. Johanna kept the engine roaring at top speed all the way to town to keep from hearing the frantic thumping behind her.

But when she switched off the engine in the street outside the hotel, she heard nothing at all. She got out and yanked open the back door with a creaking, wrenching sound, not knowing what she hoped to find.

A stench of dust and sweat flew out at her. At first she could see nothing in the hot, thick darkness. Then suddenly he appeared, sitting up and blinking at the rectangle of light in which she stood. He did not look like the same man she had put into the van. He was brown with dust from the cuffs of his overalls to his shaggy hair. His eyes were glazed. He made no move to get out, but waited silently to be pulled, feet first, from the van.

He spoke not a word to his daughter as she led

him, untied, up the steps of the hotel. And he said nothing to her again for the rest of his life.

While Johanna waited for her emigration papers to clear in the days that followed, Louw went on long unsteady walks about the town. It had changed since the times he had occasionally come shopping on Saturday mornings. The main street was paved now as far as the post office, which marked the boundary between the European and African parts of town. There were fewer shops in the European section, and fewer white people. None of them seemed to speak Louw's language, only English. The shops had big glass windows where new flags were displayed—bold red, green, and black flags proclaiming the nation's independence. Their presence was unobtrusive, though, beside the glitter of big white refrigerators, orange tractors, shining farm implements. Louw walked the streets with glazed eyes. He could not be sure if be had ever seen this town before.

In the post office, the Africans no longer stood aside to let the Europeans step to the front of the queue. Though the bakery still gave off scents of cinnamon and Scottish shortbread, Louw could hear the murmur of Kiswahili mixed with the British ladies' chatter. He had no letters to collect or money to buy cakes. He was only in town to wait, to wait until he could return to his land. He stopped straining his eyes to squint through doorways. His gaze passed over all the new things without noticing them, like the mindless beam of a fog light.

His behavior with the African children of the town was such that his daughter seldom dared show her face outside the hotel. The old man seemed to be preaching to them. His long white beard made some of the smaller ones think perhaps he was God. They even called him God in their language—mostly as an uneasy joke, but not entirely. God, they saw in pictures in the Mission Bookshop window, was an old white man with a long beard. Or so the Europeans believed. When, driven by hunger, the children came to the European part of town to beg, they would follow the old man about. Because he was almost blind, they would take his hand to lead him across the street if there was any traffic.

In the late afternoons, he would sit on the bottom step of the hotel and recite verses of scripture to the children, patting their dusty heads as if they were puppies. They weren't afraid of him. The tiny ones touched his white skin and beard, to see what he felt like. Then they pulled back their hands and stared at them, screaming sometimes with delight and terror. The old man would stroke his beard and crack his toothless grin. He told them stories, tales of the brave ox-wagon pioneers of his homeland who had slaughtered many a heathen Zulu in their mission to open up the land for civilization. Like his ancestors, he had found a new land and made it his; he had reaped abundance from the wilderness

The children listened hypnotized by the strange sputtering sounds his words made, even though, since they were Afrikaans words, the children could understand nothing of what he said.

And the old man gave them things, to make them come back and see him. Johanna would not allow him to have money, so he had to give them some of the things he found in his old suitcases she had thrown into the van at the farm. Sometimes the gift was the empty frame of a magnifying glass, sometimes a handful of empty Shotgun shells, or a bristleless hairbrush, or half of a blacksmith's tongs. The children stared at these things, not knowing what they could be. But they accepted them, laughing, in the manner in which they were given: formally, with both hands cupped. Later they tried to sell the gifts, but could never find any buyers, and eventually they lost them. But sometimes the old man would have stale biscuits or tiny watercress sandwiches left over from tea, so the children would always come back for more. They were always hungry.

One day the old man brought out of the hotel something that was truly extraordinary—an enormous bronze clock. The thing shone like gold in the sunlight. It was more than a foot tall, with its clawed feet resting on a black marble slab. On its top was a big round bell with a hammer attached to it. The numbers on the face were gold. They didn't look like any numbers the children had ever seen before— they were X's and V's and I's, like the characters in some strange language. The boys who were old enough to know that the thing was a clock pressed their ears against the glass face to hear the ticking. But this was not a ticking clock. It had not run for many years. The clock could still ring, though.

The old man wound a key on its back and dropped the key into the pocket of his bib overalls. He moved his hand. Suddenly the hammer began to strike the bell so fast you couldn't see it moving. The children shrieked and leapt back. They would have run away if Louw had not stopped the ringing. They closed around him again, curiously, shyly. Now the old man took hold of a boy's fingers and showed him how to pull out a button on the back. The clock rang again. Again the children screamed, but fewer of them jumped away. They all wanted to make the thing ring. Each one in turn pulled and pushed the button, making the clock ring and stop, ring and stop. People passing by paused to see what the noise was coming from. A few Africans stayed to watch, but the Europeans walked on quickly with their hands over their ears. It was a very loud clock, and it reverberated throughout the clean quiet street. Its noise made the dogs bark, and brought the English ladies out of the bakery. They clustered on the sidewalk, whispering and shaking their heads; then they ducked back inside, shutting the door behind them.

The ringing also brought Johanna out of the hotel. Holding her flapping skirts, she flew down the steps. Her slippered feet slapped the boards almost as fast as the hammer was vibrating against the bell. She ran down to the ragged boy who was holding the clock and snatched it out of his hands. Holding it against her chest, she moved her fingers frantically about on the back in search of the right button. Finally the clock went silent. You could suddenly hear car motors and people's voices in the street again.

Panting, she brushed damp gray strands of hair from her forehead and glared at her father. Her cheeks burned. She had to put down the clock to pull the old man to his feet. When she gripped him under the arm he staggered backwards, clutching at the air to keep from toppling over. The children, who had never seen an old man handled this way, gaped in horror as the woman tugged him up the steps, cursing in the strange sputtering language.

The hotel door closed behind them. The children again approached the steps where the clock sat. The boy who had first touched it pulled out the button and waited. Again the clock rang, but only for a moment. The sound faded. The hammer quivered slower and slower. Finally it stopped moving, its head cocked away from the bell.

Another boy tried it, but the clock remained silent. He put it down on the step where the woman had left it, and they all stared at it.

Soon the children drifted away. The younger ones were afraid of the clock, the older ones were angry and didn't want it, even to sell.

Johanna, appearing at the top of the steps, pushed the door open hard to frighten away any children who might be lurking there. She found the clock perched on the bottom step, its glass face shining like a mirror in the sunlight.

The next time anyone saw the old man, he was sitting very still and silent on the terrace next to the hotel door. His daughter sat facing him in silence, her elbows resting on the table. She was slowly shredding a paper napkin between her fingers. When the children walked by, the old man cracked his toothless smile, and lifted his hand briefly from the armrest of his chair. The gesture appeared to cost him a great effort. He did not come down to give the children gifts or let them touch him. And of course they did not venture up onto the terrace where the white people sat.

A few days later, when the children passed the hotel, the old man and the woman were not on the terrace.

That afternoon, the bell of the old Dutch church rang slowly. The children saw a van rolling out of town, and followed its trail of red dust to the graveyard. Standing behind the bars that enclosed the shaggy grass and stones, they watched silently as a big box was lowered into a hole in the ground. They knew it was him, the old man, for they saw the woman, his daughter, standing near the hole. They watched to see if she would weep or cry out or beat her chest, but she did none of these things. She merely wiped her forehead while a young man read aloud from a black book. When he was finished, she climbed back into the van. Slamming the door, she started the engine with a roar and drove off toward the south.

The children stayed to watch two African men shovel dirt into the hole. They stared at the hole's wooden marker and at the letters on it which, had they been able to read them, would have been too far away to make out. Then the children drifted away.

Thereafter, when they passed the hotel, they walked quickly until well beyond it. But always, at least one of them would glance back up at the terrace, to see if the old man had come back.

One of the children woke up screaming in the night because of a dream. He saw the old man climbing out of his box in the graveyard and lurching back toward the town with an enormous gold clock under his arm.

AN AMOROUS CONSPIRACY

BY CAPTAIN CHARLES BLACKBURN

(In 1882, an American spiritual seeker in India, whose name appears above, wrote of one of his adventures, changing his own name to "Ben" and that of his British lady friend—she happened to be married—to "Daisy." As if the tale were fiction, he told it in the third person. He retained the true names of two beings from the spirit world whom he had encountered in his travels: the captain's wise mentor named Master Moreya, and Devi, the shade of a princess who seemed to have formed an attachment to the handsome, bearded, turbaned Master Moreya. She had recently left her home in a desert temple to accompany him and the captain to the Himalayas. Both spirit beings, of course, were invisible to the mortals, including the author, though he could often feel their presence and intuit their messages. The

captain's description, included below, may serve as an introduction to his story. . . .)

On the Great Hindustan Highway on the slope of Mount Jakko, a cuckoo chirps in a tall deodar pine. You listen, and if you're British (as most of the residents of this Himalayan hill station called Simla are) the bird song will magically transport you to a cool, damp English garden. At the same time, you hear the faint tweeting of a tribesman's wooden flute. It's a sound so Indian, so utterly un-British, so weirdly *other*, that it could be the laughter of pagan demons rising on air currents from the valley below. Such dramatic contrast—West: East—causes a sharp ache deep in your breast. Soon the dissonance becomes intolerable: you'll have to choose to be enchanted either by the cuckoo or the flute.

And if you're British, the bird will win out. From now on you will embrace everything English with the ardor of someone falling in love with an old flame who after an absence appears even more radiant than she was before. You become much more enthusiastic, more sentimental, more patriotic—more English—than you ever were at home.

And now as you climb toward the town, every Indian you see becomes merely an exotic supporting character in the delightful English drama in which you and your kind are the star performers. Hindu ladies in sarees are playing sweepers and ayahs (nursemaids). The pagan hill tribesmen, with their nose rings and goatskin hair ornaments and woven reed back-packs, act in the roles of bearers; they carry Crosse & Blackwell jam jars, tins of Scottish salmon, Fortnum's and Mason's tea cakes, and all the beloved symbols of home and hearth to be set out as props upon your stage. The hills on either side become the folds of green velvet curtains that frame Himalayan peaks so high and distant that they look two-dimensional—as if drawn on a vast canvas backdrop: a jagged horizon of snowy white, painted below a ceiling of dazzling blue. Superb! you say aloud, feeling the invigorating cool air rush into your lungs. And you rub your hands together with anticipation of a marvelous English holiday.

But if you are an American spiritualist seeker? You try somehow, as I have, to synthesize the sounds of cuckoo and flute, of West and East. It is a challenge I am looking forward eagerly—optimistically—ardently—

(*The captain did not finish this description. His story continues....*)

Princess Devi was having too good a time mixing invisibly in the lives of mortals to re-enter the normal death-and-rebirth cycle. As a higher being, Master Moreya—Ben's astral guide—might have condemned her reckless behavior. But the Master occasionally allowed his spirit colleagues and himself lapses from perfection.

Now, as fortune would have it, Devi was in Simla at the same time that Ben and his lady friend Daisy were visiting the hill station. One evening after her arrival, Devi parted the curtains of Daisy's chalet to watch the two mortals approaching along a moonlit path. Moreya joined her at the window. Wrapping her silver saree around her shoulders, she looked out over the Anandale Valley to enjoy the sky's starry serenity.

Ben and Daisy were coming from Simla's little

theater where they'd attended a performance of *Walpole* by Sir Edward Bullwer-Lytton. During the interval, Daisy agreed that it was an uplifting work, but as the second act droned on, Ben heard a faint warbling beside him and had to squeeze Daisy's elbow to awaken her. Suppressing a laugh, she laid a gloved hand over his. The glove became warm, then hot, then damp; at the end of the act, the pair fairly burst out of the theater.

The Simla roadways had been hung with fairy lights that blurred and rippled in the fog. "Like a fête!" Daisy remarked as she swung her arms gaily at her sides. Floating behind, Moreya and Devi saw a picture form in Ben's head—a farm-boy (himself) approaching a county fair, his eyes growing wide at the spectacle of tents and flares and turbaned barkers. And calliope music . . . now he heard some drifting up from the ice-palace where ladies and gentlemen were "rinking"—Simla's favorite sport this season. As Ben caught sight of the skaters gliding around the gleaming floor, he felt that his movements were fluid and effortless, too. Daisy looked unusually graceful herself—even girlish, despite her spectacles and plump form—as she moved her feet in rhythm to the calliope's beat.

She and Ben had felt slightly brazen all evening appearing at the theater together, though Daisy's husband had given her permission to attend cultural events with Ben while he remained behind in Bombay. No one took the slightest notice of them. "We're too old to get gossiped about," Daisy whispered to Ben. The "poodle-faking"—flirting—that Simla was famous for took place among the dashing young officers and the "fishing fleet" girls who'd come out from England looking for husbands. Further along the path, the music faded and the landscape was lit only by the moon careening across the sky through gossamer shreds of cloud. Now that Ben and Daisy were alone together, Moreya could see that both of them were feeling a little shy. Until tonight, their embraces had been quickly stolen and all too brief.

"There's something faintly . . . divine about all this space!" Daisy said in a hushed voice. "Doesn't it seem that we're being watched by strange, powerful forces?"

"Yes. I understand why the Masters choose to live in the Himalayas," Ben said. Luminescent white, the peaks appeared above the dark foothills like enormous icebergs. The moon seemed to take its glow from their light, and not vice versa.

"I feel currents in the air," she whispered. "Listen—"

And Ben heard the faint roar of wildly rushing steams rising and pulsing through the darkness.

"You know, I hoped for something gayer at the theater," she said. "A costume-drama, with gowns and robes and so forth. D'you like them?"

"Oh, yes. I used to act in plays myself, in school."

"My father never allowed me near any theatrical events. He was a clergymen. He dressed me all in gray, like a grown woman." Daisy sighed. "I couldn't act in the pantomimes other children got up, but I liked to hide behind the hedge to watch them. . . ."

Just then, the pair heard a shuffling sound in the darkness, and turned to see a man carrying a lantern dangling from the end of a long stick. Behind him two men trotted along pulling a rickshaw. Its oilcloth had been drawn up against the evening damp; as the moonlight struck it, the vehicle glittered like a tiny enchanted carriage. Devi—unseen, of course—was perched on the hood, lending it her own silver radiance. Moreya joined her there, and she gave him a certain look.

"Amazing—something straight from a stage production!" Ben whispered. Daisy squeezed his arm.

Ben hailed the rickshaw and helped her to climb in. It was a one-seater, so he walked beside it. Before him, the silhouetted figure with the bobbing lantern glided along the path, casting out a faint cone of light. It illuminated swaying pine-boughs, wild mountain rhododendrons, tiny streams that trickled musically beside the path. Daisy laid her hand on the wooden armrest, and as Ben strolled beside her, he held it. She'd removed her glove; her fingers felt cool. Her hand made no movement, yet he sensed an energy in it, as if it were about to take off into the air and soar like a white bird into the valley below.

He walked on until at Daisy's gate the vehicle halted. Its hood rose as Moreya and Devi stepped off into the air. Daisy alighted, too, and Ben paid the rickshaw-pullers.

"Well. . . ." Daisy stepped through the gate. "Here we are. Thank you ever so much for a lovely evening."

"No need to thank me. But must you retire so early?"

"I—I should—"

Just then Ben touched his eye. It had started watering.

"What's the matter?" Daisy asked.

He leaned over, squinting. "I seem to have caught a gnat."

"Let me look—" Daisy stood on tiptoe, but at that moment a cloud passed over the moon like a billowing silver saree, and she could see nothing.

Ben blinked. "If I could just bathe it for a moment—"

"Of course you could—"

And so they proceeded up the flagstone walk toward the verandah. The watchman ran toward them bearing a flaming torch. He escorted them to the door, then slipped off into the shadows, his flambeau leaving a smoking trail in the air. Daisy lit a paraffin lamp, and the foyer flickered into view.

Ben carried the lamp for her through the house to the wash stand in the kitchen yard. Dipping a cloth in a pail of water, she dabbed at his eye. The gnat—Ben later suspected that it was a microscopic elemental spirit—was evicted. He wiped his face on the first towel he found. Then, seeing his reflection in a mirror on the wall, he discovered that he'd been transformed into a Moor.

"Oh, no! I used that towel to clean up some powdered henna I spilled!" Daisy laughed. "Why Ben, you look so—so swarthy. . . ."

"So I do. All I need is a turban!" Still chuckling, he smeared the rest of his face with reddish brown color from the towel.

She leaned her forehead against his chest. "My brave rajah," she giggled. "Oh, d'you know what? This house is supposed to be haunted—I just found out!"

"Tell me about this!"

"Well, a beautiful English memsahib was supposed to have fallen in love with an Indian prince here. He was ever so handsome and dashing, but something of a rake, I'm afraid. He went off, and she thought he'd deserted her. She pined away for love!"

"For love. . . ." Ben stood very still. "I think I feel a certain astral energy."

"Do you?" She pressed closer to him. "Oh, so do I!"

He did feel a presence in the air—as well he might, since Princess Devi was hovering nearby. You can guess who it was who'd snatched the powder-dusted towel from the bottom of the laundry hamper and placed it on top of the stack for him to find.

"The energy seems to be coming from the house—from upstairs," Ben whispered. "I've developed a sensitivity about these things. But I've never been presented with an occasion to test them before."

Daisy smiled. "Shall we go looking for the lovelorn memsahib?"

"We must." Ben wrapped his arm around her waist. Leaving the lantern in the yard, they tiptoed into the parlor. Its furniture was covered in ghostly dust-cloths for the night. They moved stealthily along a hall. Devi flew from gas-jet to gas-jet, blocking each one, but she needn't have bothered. Knowing that astral entities de-materialize upon contact with luminous energy, Ben made no move to light the gas.

The stairs creaked as the two went up. Daisy clung to Ben's arm. They stopped abruptly, seeing a human figure lying on the hall carpet; it was only the children's ayah asleep in front of the nursery door. Daisy checked on the girls, then shut the door softly behind her. Stepping over the supine nursemaid, they tiptoed on. Moonlight streamed through the window at the far end of the hall, making streaks on the walls like splashes of silver.

Ben slowed, half-closing his eyes. "I can feel something . . . very near," he whispered. "Perhaps in here." He opened a door. It made a strange squealing sound, as if unwilling to admit mortal strangers to its depths. He took a deep breath and plunged into the darkness.

He didn't plunge far. It was a linen cupboard. His forehead struck a shelf. His pince-nez fell to the floor. Daisy, sweating in her purple velvet dress, helped him look for it. Since the space was so confined, Moreya and Devi heard a great many grunts and giggles before the spectacles could be found. As they left the cupboard, Devi planted a certain idea in Daisy's mind.

"Take a towel," Daisy whispered to Ben, and he did. She snatched something from a hook before she left.

"What have you got?"

"Won't tell!" Daisy fluttered her hand at her side. "I think I feel the energy...." She opened another door. This one made no squeal at all; it seemed to sway back even before her fingertips touched its surface, as if some force were pulling it open for her—which of course it was. Devi flew off to perch on the bedstead, where Moreya joined her.

Ben examined the maroon towel in his hands. "Ah, a turban," he said, catching on. Daisy helped him wrap it round his head, fastening it with a pin over his forehead. Then she pulled a curtain from its rod, leaving the gauze liner fluttering in the breeze, and wrapped the heavy material around Ben's shoulders.

He pulled her close. "Velvet against velvet," he murmured. "Such magnetic energy."

And they did make sparks as they embraced in the darkness. "Wait—the memsahib would have worn a special costume for her prince," Daisy whispered. She vanished into the dressing room.

Gazing out the window, Ben suddenly heard the faint, haunting notes of a native flute rise from the valley below. Then he turned, hearing the whisper of cloth behind him. Daisy reappeared, looking splendid. She was wearing what she'd snatched from the linen cupboard: the ayah's daytime saree of thin, translucent cotton. The light from the lantern in the yard below flickered in the window like a lovely footlight. Daisy seemed to step out of an oil painting of a Victorian lady in romantic native costume. Her hair rippled to her shoulders. From the saree's bodice her plump white bosom spilled, quivering with each dainty step. Ben could hear her thighs whispering inside the saree.

"The perfect maharanee," he gasped.

"Except for the specs!" She laughed, gazing at the big framed mirror over the bureau. "But I need them to see you, Ben Sahib."

In the mirror, Ben's own glasses made him look, with his new turban, like a distinguished Hindu pandit. A—dare he think it?—a powerful Master!

He took Daisy in his arms. Snatches of music from the rink reached them on the night air. They danced together round and round the room. Dipping, swirling, they glanced over their shoulders at their reflections in the mirror. The light was dim enough to hide their age, kindly revealing them as a young English maharanee and her dashing swarthy prince, reunited at last in the ballroom of the Mogul palace of their dreams.

Now, many have wondered if sensual love occurs between beings in the world of spirits. It does, but it's usually ethereal, like two moonbeams passing through each other, with almost no tactile sensations. Only occasional spiritual shivers ignite the dust motes to remind the astral beings of their former fleshy selves. But when such beings are able to take possession of the bodies of mortals . . . well, then there is physical love between the spirits, indeed.

Moreya, it must be said, had been focusing some powerful energy currents on Princess Devi for some time, noticing her almond eyes, her long black tresses, her slim round hips. Though she was over two hundred years old, she looked not a day older than eighteen, and exceedingly luscious. Of course she had noticed Moreya, as well: his distinguished beard, his burning gaze, his breathtakingly handsome presence undiminished by his own three centuries. As Ben and Daisy danced together, Moreya and Devi gave each other a meaningful glance . . . and dove deep beneath their hosts' costumes.

Perhaps you've read the classic work, the *Kamasutra* (both Daisy and Ben secretly had), and recall the colorful couplings depicted in their pages. Not all of the positions were possible for partners of our lovers' girth and age. But with a certain amount of stretching, grunting, giggling and oofing, an heroic number of exotic postures were enacted in those shafts of moonlight upon the bed. Feet kicked high in the air, arms flailed ecstatically, sarees and robes tangled and rippled and dropped to the floor. Daisy cried out words she never knew were in her vocabulary. Ben chuckled. Spectacles clinked; then they, too, dropped away. The lovers groped blindly. They bounced, they burrowed. They became a single thirsty beast with a head at each end. They became horse and rider (Devi's favorite). They became roaring, mewing jungle cats (Moreya's personal preference). Spotted all over from the damp powder, they purred like leopards rolling in soft, tropical grasses.

Devi and Moreya could have kept them at it all night, but they took pity on their corporeal forms.

As Daisy lay panting on Ben's chest, Devi closed her own eyelids, too.

Later, fluttering upwards, Moreya and Devi loosed the bed's mosquito netting from its frame and let it fall in a translucent canopy around Ben and Daisy. Soon the astral lovers were gently rocking together in a wicker chair to the rhythm of their hosts' musical snores.

Did Daisy really need to be prompted that night by the mischievous Indian princess? Did Ben need any inspiration from Moreya?

Probably not. But astral beings need to have a lark now and then, too.

LADY OF THE LAKE

In a cracked sepia-toned photograph, dated 1910—the first picture of her that I have—my mother sits on the gate of a horse-drawn wagon leaning back into a pile of hay. Her legs, covered in a long gingham dress, dangle over the back. I can imagine her smiling prettily a moment ago, but when she sees the camera, she stretches her lips in a contorted grimace. Her arms rise, the wings of a half-mad angel about to fly into the lens.

At twelve, her age then, I'd have enjoyed going for a hayride with a girl capable of defying an adult with a camera. I'm skinny and pale but there is nothing about me that might cause her to recoil from me. It never occurs to either of us then that I could have anything to do with that extraordinary look on her face.

As the wagon bumps along the dirt road, she tells

me how hard it is to find time to read when she has so many little brothers to care for, so many farm animals to feed and clean up after. The people in her family aren't any more interesting to talk to than the cows and chickens. Brushing straw away from her face, she talks about girls in books who ride *on* horses, not behind them.

"I don't know how I ever got into my family either," I tell her. "I feel like a monster."

I wait for her to give me an icy look and move away from me, but she doesn't. She lies back with her head close to mine and wrinkles her nose at the small white clouds spattered like chicken droppings across the Kansas sky.

"There are better places in books," she says after a while, half-closing her eyes. "I want to live in a castle on an island in the middle of a lake, with no little children or animals around—maybe one dog, a graceful greyhound, but no more." She'd have nothing to do, she says, but go for long walks and stare off into the mist and listen to the lake lapping at the shore.

I sink into the straw. She lies back too, her arms raised, wings again, gliding. Twilight falls around us like soft summer blankets. The road grows dark as we bump along. Waves of high corn lap at the wagon's sides. As she recites verses from her favorite poem, *The Lady of the Lake,* by Sir Walter Scott, the wooden wheels squeak in rhythm beneath us. *"Harp of the North . . . the wizard note has not been touched in vain . . . silent be no more . . . enchantress, wake again. . . ."*

* * *

In a 1915 photograph, she is seventeen. Dressed in a middy blouse and long skirt, she holds a stack of books against her chest. Her future adult features are recognizable—the determined smile, the quizzical raised eyebrows, the round cheeks not yet puffy. Her lips are slightly parted, forming a sound just as the camera clicks. I stare hard at the photo and try to hear a teenager's high voice coming from her lips. What was she about to say on that day in 1915?

At seventeen, I'm more solitary than her, but we seem to have become friends at high school. I'm still pale and thin—a moody, artistic look, she tells me. She is constantly, frantically on the move: debating society, yearbook, student government, literary magazine. With all those activities, she's sure that she'll win a scholarship to college. In class, while I secretly study a music score hidden under my desk top, she answers all the teacher's questions and waits for more, smiling confidently.

But in the end, her scholarship does not come through. The day she gets the news, we go to an empty classroom late in the afternoon. I gaze out the window as if I can see New York City and ocean voyages in my future. She is wearing her middy blouse; her hair, unpinned and chaotic, blazes with the sunlight behind it. She sits at a desk by the window and drops her face in her hands. Her fingernails dig into her temples. I wait for her to speak, watching her lips.

"I've rehearsed speeches in the barn while I milked the cows," she says in a hollow, whispery voice. "I've smiled through endless meetings till my teeth ached. And my best hasn't been good enough. *Not good enough!*"

"It's just that the school's no good, the town's too small," I tell her. "It's not your fault."

She glares out at the stubbled cornfields. Then

she turns to me, her mouth half open, and for an instant she looks as if she has just released a wordless screech that has torn the lungs out of her. Her face is severely composed now, but I'm sure I can hear the echo of her voice reverberating along the walls of the empty classroom like fast-beating wings, as if birds were flapping up the dusty plaster trying to escape. With a swipe of her wrist, she removes the tears from her eyes, and the sound vanishes as if it had never been made. Perhaps it never was.

But it lingers on her lips in the photograph.

When I leave town, she looks very serious as she tells me good-bye. I'm surprised that she has a going-away present for me—a book about great composers. I wish I had a gift for her.

*   *   *

There are no pictures of my mother at college—she did finally get there. But it was a small place, uncultured. She had to wait on tables in a sorority house. Her poverty showed like a rash. After two years she left for New York, where by now she knew the money was, and the real culture. She was certain that they were the same thing.

Only one photograph survives from the years in New York (1919-1932). It is of a brick city building: a stoop, a door, curtained windows. No people, just a building. On the back of the photo, in quavery letters: *Bank Street.* My mother's handwriting.

I thought at first that it was my parents' apartment. My mother once told me that they lived in Greenwich Village for many years because they were saving money for a house in the country; they were certainly not bohemians—my father worked for an accounting firm. They did go to speakeasies, not realizing, my mother insisted, that they were supporting gangsters. They danced the Charleston. "Oh, your father was a marvelous dancer, once," she told me.

I have lived in Greenwich Village, and can picture Bank Street. I think now that the building in the photograph is the one where Edna St. Vincent Millay lived. I'm sure that my mother would have been more likely to save a picture of it than of her own apartment. When she found out that the poet lived close by, she climbed five flights of stairs to get her to autograph one of her books. Thirty years later, she told the story at cocktail parties in the Connecticut house, but she never got any response—none of the guests knew who Edna St. Vincent Millay was. The signed book remained locked in a glass cabinet in the living room.

* * *

I'm at Edna's apartment when a young woman arrives at the door with a book in her hand. She stands on the landing, her cheeks flushed, her mouth slightly open—she's winded from climbing the stairs. When she smiles, her lips widen almost prettily, then retreat to press against her teeth.

"I hope I'm not disturbing Miss Millay," she says. "I've seen her coming and going on the street. You see, I live just three doors down. . . ." Her voice trails off as she looks at me.

I don't fit into the elegant scene she imagined, pale and unshaven as I am, and barefoot at eleven in the morning, as if I might have just gotten out of bed, perhaps with the poet herself. In fact I've been up for several hours scribbling away at the score for an opera I'm trying to write; I wish I could go back to it now.

"I expect you want to leave off some of your poems for her to read," I say. Sometimes people do that.

"Oh, no, I'd just like her to sign my book. Her book, I mean."

A nervous laugh escapes; she pushes it back into her mouth with a white-gloved hand as if she'd just sneezed. She's got on her best clothes, a gray two piece outfit with a loop of artificial pearls and flat shoes; it's what she thinks sophisticated Eastern college graduates wear. She has no idea that Edna fled Vassar to escape girls who looked like this. Has a dreary secretarial job or a husband who hates poetry pressed those lines into her forehead?

"You can come in," I tell her, stepping back inside the doorway.

"I'm afraid I'm disturbing her at work."

"The person from Porlock? I doubt it. Anyway, there's so many better things to be afraid of."

Her eyebrow rises quizzically—I do say odd things sometimes. "I know," she says finally.

She walks in and stands before the window. Despite her city clothes, she moves as if she's used to tramping across frozen fields in a storm. She knows how to wrestle a calf out of a snowdrift: good training, in a way, for presenting herself unannounced at the court of the Snow Princess to ask for and get, against all odds, an autograph. Slowly turning her face, she bathes in the dusty beige light that slants through the window. She gazes at the water color landscapes, the antique chairs, the silver candlesticks—for candles burnt at both ends, perhaps she is thinking. The wall beside the window is red brick turned to the texture of chamois by the soft light. I watch her inspect with delight the piles of books and manuscripts on the piano.

Suddenly I hear Edna stirring in the next room, and hope that she won't be haughty or smell of liquor when she comes in. Then, dispelling worries, she wafts through her doorway, all soft wools and white delicate skin. A silk scarf flows round her neck and down her shoulder. Her hair is a lovely red blur. She picks up a pile of papers from the piano, pursing her lips to whistle a tune to herself.

"Hello?" she says, suddenly noticing the visitor. Her eyelashes flick up, and she splashes a look at the woman: Are you interesting? Will you amuse me? Will you have lovely small white breasts? Will your story give my heart an ache and a poem? All these questions in a vibrating instant; then the lashes drop with an answer audible to me but fortunately not to the visitor: No? Oh well, never mind—

The visitor's cheeks flush. A beautiful young woman has never looked at her this way before—probably no one has. "I am Marion Langley," she says, finally reassembling her rehearsed greeting. "My husband and I live just down the block. I have often seen you, I've read all your poems, I've admired. . . ."

Edna smiles pleasantly until she's finished talking, then reaches out her hand to take the book the woman has been hugging to her chest. "It's very sweet of you to come," Edna says. She takes up a pen and scribbles on the fly leaf. "Now I'm afraid I have to rush—" She gives the book back, puts on her cloche hat with both hands, throws me a kiss. Then she is out the door, stuffing papers into her purse as she drops out of sight down the stairwell.

Edna, too, says "I'm afraid"—I hadn't noticed that before. I'm grateful for everything I learn about her. I sit down on the couch beside my notebook, sorry that Edna dismissed Marion Langley so quickly.

The woman gazes out onto the landing, her face lifted as if she is listening to a trail of musical notes Edna has left behind her. I hear them, too, and forget for a moment that it's just the pianist practicing downstairs. A trace of Edna's perfume floats in the air, a pale purple tint among the beige sunbeams.

"This. . . ." Marion Langley pauses as an arpeggio flutters past. "*This* is what I came to New York for. It's like standing in the middle of a poem." She turns to me. "You know, things so seldom live up to one's expectations. When I first came to New York, I thought it would all be like this, but it never has been. Until now." She holds the book in both hands, one wrist cradling it from beneath. I have a feeling that for her, things never will be like this again. I think, also, that she has no one to show her treasure to.

"Let's see it." I lean forward.

She opens the cover of the book and holds it out to me. Her hair falls over her cheek; she brushes it back impatiently, watching my face to see my reaction.

To Mary Ann, Best Wishes, Edna St. V. Millay.

The corners of her mouth dip down, try to rise again. "She must be thinking of more important things."

I invent. "There's someone called Mary Ann in the poem she's working on. Edna gets preoccupied. . . ."

"Oh." Her eyes light up. The mistake in the flyleaf has new meaning, a special value now. She closes the book carefully and smiles at me. "Are you, uh . . . her husband?"

"Not me." I grin. "I'm temporary."

"Oh." She's trying not to stare at my bare feet, which are dirty on the bottom. "Well, you've been very kind."

"No, I'm glad you came," I say, and stand up to see her to the door. Edna's scent is faint on the landing. The piano music has stopped. Suddenly I face her. "I forget sometimes that I might be living in the middle of—something important."

"You mean you didn't realize?"

I shake my head. And I'm afraid that I don't know how much more of it there will be, or if things will ever be this way again. We shake hands good-bye. Her loop of pale pearls clicks against itself as she turns away. I wave to her from the doorway. I am suddenly lonely.

* * *

The only photograph with both my mother and father in it—the last one before I was born—is labeled June, 1940. My parents stride in light summer outfits across the deck of a cruise ship. Though they are several feet apart, their legs and arms are in exactly the same positions; they seem to be fast-marching in lock-step.

My mother has a strange expression on her face: she looks happy but spooked, a little like the girl on the back of the hay wagon. Her lips are stretched wide in amazement. She seems to be humming something, but I can't quite hear it.

I remember my mother mentioning a shipboard dance contest, and now I picture the ballroom of a ship floating midway across the Atlantic. On the night before the photo on the deck was taken, my parents are dancing at a 1920's theme party. Cutouts of flappers and Stutz Bearcats are hung at crazy angles on the walls. The revolving chandelier releases swarms of sparkling butterflies. Men dip and sway in black tuxedos; women in ball gowns throw their heads back and click their high heels on the parquet.

I am the bandleader and master of ceremonies, with my hair lying black and oily across my scalp, my smile tasting like rubber. *"Yes sir, that's my baby,"* I croon into the microphone, and waves of gaiety wash back and forth across the floor.

The dance contest is beginning. When, broke and out of luck, I first took this job in purgatory, the contests used to make me uneasy, but no longer. I come down off the bandstand and dart among the couples. I pause to admire their grace and polish. Then I kill them. When I tap a man's shoulder with my baton, the couple has to stop dancing and must leave the floor, out of the contest. The young ones go quickly. Then I search out the middle-aged men who have kept themselves trim with lifetimes of golf and polo, and women whose breakfasts of dove's milk or whatever they drink has kept them willowy. These couples I cut down with flourishes of my wand, bringing it to rest on the backs of necks like the tip of a sword blade. You. And you. And you.

The captain has given me strict orders about which couple is to win: a beaming pink-domed tycoon and his poodle-faced blonde who swirls around him in a crinoline blur. Only one other couple remains now. They are good, especially him, a tall, hawk-nosed man with a shock of gray hair rising from his forehead. The woman, middle aged, stocky, her make-up turned to plaster by cooled sweat, is fueled by champagne and a kind of ecstasy. What can be getting into her tonight? It's the cruise: it's finally being here among the kind of elegant people she could only have dreamed of during her dreary childhood. Her eyes have never flown so wide open, her feet have never kicked so high.

As the band goes into a final Charleston, I strut round and round, my baton bobbing in the air before me. I've decided to make my own choice. All eyes follow me. Ladies squeal behind gloved fingers; men stomp their feet like a crowd at a public execution.

Who is to be chopped and who spared? I half-shut my eyes, spin in place, and bring my baton down on the nearest shoulder.

Did fate decide whose? No, that was just an operatic flourish to please the audience and to deceive the captain, who glowers at me now like God in epaulets from the shadows behind the bandstand.

The murderous wand has fallen onto the tycoon. He and his drooping partner shuffle to a halt and bow briefly toward the winners.

The other couple freezes, holding hands at arms length, knees swayed, heads back. He looks as smug as I knew he would. But her face amazes me with its beauty. I snatch up the tall winner's cup and run with it across the floor, pumping it high into the air to make the applause flutter down on them like cascades of silver leaves.

Later, I roam the decks watching the phosphorescent waves roll past the ship. The captain has fired me—my roulette-wheel spin on the dance floor deceived no one—and now my wand floats somewhere on the ship's wake.

I hear voices nearby and duck behind a funnel. The winning couple passes by. She holds his arm and sings something in a high, small voice. A champagne bottle swings in her free hand. They stop. She raises her face, bathing it in the glow from the paper lanterns that bob on strings overhead. The deck tilts gently; snatches of dance music fly on the breeze with the scent of salt spray. She pulls the cup from under his arm and gazes at it. Though it is only tin—I've given away scores of the things—it seems to gleam like a silver grail. Now she fills it with champagne, raises it to her lips, then to his.

They stagger off down a corridor. I perch precariously on a railing as they rush breathlessly into their stateroom. The porthole's round glass turns them to contorted figures in a fish-eye camera lens. The man and woman fall onto the bunk, and the whole ship seems to rock. My stomach tilts; I clutch the railing tight to keep from tumbling off. One lantern remains stationary as the others sway around it: the moon.

The woman in the lens lies on her back, her gown and petticoats whispering above her white legs. She spreads her knees wide apart as if to absorb the moonbeams into her womb. The man kneels over her, his suspenders fallen. He raises the bottle. Champagne splashes over her thighs, sizzles on her mound of moon-ignited hair. She screams, laughs, the bubbles bursting, bursting, inside her. The bottle falls empty to the floor and rolls across a moonbeam.

I turn away quickly—I lose my balance on the railing—I tilt backwards, and plunge toward the waves. The spray rises fast. As the phosphorescence closes around me, I hear a woman's voice singing: *"Yes, sir, that's my baby, that's my baby now...."*

The next morning, they go for a stroll on deck, feeling sheepish, hung over, amazed. When the couples from the dance nod at them, my parents smile and nod back, shivering with the thrill of their social success. I can hear my mother humming the song the bandleader crooned into his silver microphone. The camera clicks, freezing them in that strange lock-stepped stroll.

Do they know that what they have done the night before will keep them locked to each other for another twenty years? No, no. In the brilliant sunlight of a cloudless day on the open sea, the notion that a child might have been conceived on moonbeams and champagne cannot have occurred to them.

* * *

The next photo, with a hospital stamp on the back, is dated February 1941, nine months after the cruise. My mother is sitting in a white bed looking pale and dazed. Strands of hair fall to her forehead like gray cobwebs. Her lips cringe back.

A bundle with a puckered face at one end lies beside her on the sheet. Thin arms and legs protrude crookedly from it like the tentacles of some creature snatched from the briny deep.

Me.

No wonder she is dazed. I am the surprise of my parents' lives. My mother is 43, my father 46. Can I really be their child? My eyes are squeezed tight. I appear about to yowl—I can feel it coming on. So can my mother, from the look on her face. I try to imagine us opening our mouths wide in unison and yowling up a storm loud enough to sink an ocean liner. But my mother just sits there in exhausted silence. I lie squirming with astonishment.

I have stopped her life, and begun my own.

AT SARATOGA, *1985*

FOR DAN AND FOR LANA

On a warm summer day, I rowed my children across a shallow lake where some other small children had died a hundred years before.

My son, just recently past their ages, knew the story. I watched his face struggle as he spotted them beneath the water, lying on their backs, wrapped in weed shrouds. The plants swayed in the current, reaching toward the surface.

My daughter, younger, not knowing, said she saw green hills under the boat, and we were flying above them. She pointed to the clouds floating beside us on the water. My son saw me smile, and nodded.

Resting the oars, I listened to my live children talk in low voices against the stillness. The voices hovered around the boat, making ripples that fanned out toward the shore where the trees watched us like tall angels. The shadows of their branches settled over the water: huge, soft wings.

The boat glided on.

"Faster," my son said, watching the weeds.

"Slower," I whispered, as the clouds' reflections broke open before the bow.

My whisper scuttled over the wake: a water bug.

That day, the surface held.

But sometimes I feel the current rushing past me. I reach for the oars to row my children across the sky.

BVG